Dear Reader,

We've all had those days when nothing seems to go our way. Days when our work is full of jerks, PMS, hair that won't behave and cars that don't run. "If *we* were in charge," we say, "things would be different!"

My heroine Phoebe Frame has had one day too many like this and decides to do something about it. Writing in first person, I felt as though I was an observer along for the ride, taking dictation as Phoebe set out to exact revenge and make the kind of life she's always wanted for herself. And believe me, I never knew what Phoebe was going to do next!

I hope you enjoy reading about "our" adventure! Let me know what you think of this story—I always love to hear from readers. E-mail me at cindi@cindimyers.com. And stop by my Web site at www.cindimyers.com to see what's new with me.

Happy reading!

Cindi Myers

"Get your hands off of me!"

"You're the one who ran into me, lady." He was quite tall and, in a better mood, I probably would have thought he was handsome.

We glared at each other, neither one wanting to be the first to look away. However, as much fun as this was, I had tons of work to finish.

The thing to do was act calm and collected. Ms. Cool. "If you're here to see the doctor, his office is back there." I pointed down the hallway.

"Actually, I'm looking for a Phoebe Frame." The man glanced around. "Maybe you could point me in the right direction and I promise to stay out of your way."

"Phoebe Frame?" Ooh, this day was improving by leaps and bounds...not. "I'm Phoebe." I cleared my throat. "And you are...?"

"Jeff Fischer. My friends call me Jeff, but you can call me Mr. Fischer."

Wonderful. This was the software specialist I would be working with—closely. Young, too good-looking and a delightful attitude. Could things possibly get better?

What Phoebe Wants

Cindi Myers

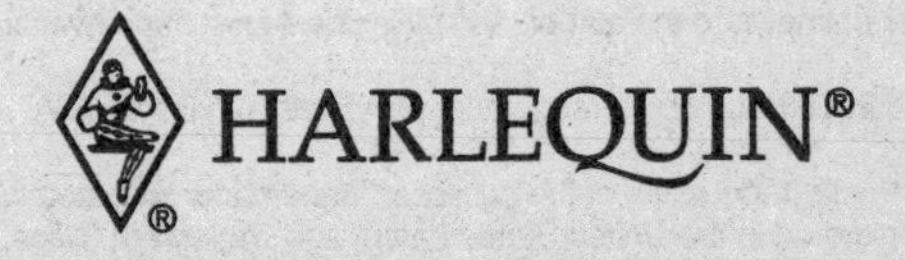

TORONTO • NEW YORK • LONDON
AMSTERDAM • PARIS • SYDNEY • HAMBURG
STOCKHOLM • ATHENS • TOKYO • MILAN • MADRID
PRAGUE • WARSAW • BUDAPEST • AUCKLAND

ISBN 0-373-44194-0

WHAT PHOEBE WANTS

This edition published by arrangement with Harlequin Books S.A.

www.eHarlequin.com

Printed in U.S.A.

ABOUT THE AUTHOR

Cindi Myers believes in love at first sight, good chocolate, cold champagne, that people who don't like animals can't be trusted and that God obviously has a sense of humor. She also believes in writing fun, sexy romances about people she hopes readers will fall in love with. In addition to writing, Cindi enjoys reading, quilting, gardening, hiking and downhill skiing. She lives in the Rocky Mountains of Colorado with her husband (whom she met on a blind date and agreed to marry six weeks later) and two spoiled dogs.

Books by Cindi Myers

HARLEQUIN FLIPSIDE
10—LIFE ACCORDING TO LUCY

HARLEQUIN TEMPTATION
902—IT'S A GUY THING!
935—SAY YOU WANT ME

HARLEQUIN BLAZE
82—JUST 4 PLAY
118—RUMOR HAS IT

For Pam Hopkins who never gave up on this one.

And special thanks to Wanda Ottewell
for giving Phoebe a chance.

1

MY GRANDMOTHER ALWAYS TOLD ME, you make your own luck. As if luck was something that could be baked like a cake or sewn like a shirt. Of course, my cakes could be used as first base down at the ballpark, and my ninth-grade home-ec class voted me "girl most likely to do bodily harm with a sewing machine." This could explain why I haven't had much luck lately, of any kind.

Which would you say is worse: being dumped by your husband who then takes up with a twenty-four-year-old cocktail waitress who has a stomach tight enough to bounce quarters off, or sitting in a cubicle that smells of cigar smoke and sweat, listening to a shiny-faced car salesman try to make you a "deal"?

Having recently endured both, I'd have to say it's something of a draw. The whole sorry business with my husband dragged on longer, but in its own way, the ordeal with the car salesman was just as tedious.

"Now, I know a woman like you is concerned about finding something dependable." The salesman nodded sagely and gave me a toothy grin. He had a bad comb-over and his deodorant had long since packed up and hitched a ride out of town. "I mean, what good is a great deal on a vehicle if it leaves you in the lurch?"

Left me in the lurch. That's what Steve did when he walked out. Just calmly packed his bags and said, "I know you don't want me here if I'm not happy." As if his leaving was all about his concern for me, and not about his own pathetic midlife crisis.

"You see what I'm saying, Ms. Frame? My only concern is that you leave here today happy."

There was that word again—happy. At this point in my life, I was beginning to think the whole pursuit of happiness shtick was highly overrated. "I just need something that will get me where I'm going and doesn't cost more than six thousand dollars." I twisted the straps of my purse in my hand.

The salesman made a face as if he'd just sucked a lemon. "Six thousand. Now, I don't know if we're gonna find much for six thousand." He leaned toward me, his yellowing teeth looming large in my vision. "Do you have a trade-in?"

I blinked. "A trade-in?"

"Another car? Do you have another car to trade in?"

"Yes. It's...uh, it's parked down the street." The maroon Ford Probe had died at the corner of Anderson and Alameda, smoke spewing from under the hood. An alarming sequence of pings and rattles issued from the engine before it gave a last gasp and simply quit altogether. I had sat there for a long moment, head on the steering wheel, too disgusted to waste tears. Then I'd gathered up my purse and keys and started walking.

Walking is a relative term in Houston in late August. It was more like swimming through the heavy, humid air. Heat radiated up from the pavement, through the soles of my sandals. Sweat pooled in the small of my back and my hair clung damply to my forehead. As I walked, I tried to think of new epithets for Steve, who had driven away from me in a brand new black Lexus, leaving me with the twelve-year-old Ford.

I'd started alphabetically, with addlepated asshole and was up to middle-aged midget-brain when I saw the sign for Easy Motors. That was it. I'd buy a new car. Or at least one that was newer than the recently departed Ford.

The salesman—the nameplate on his desk said his name was Hector—grabbed a form off the corner of the desk and began to write. "So what are you trading in?"

"It's a 1990 Ford Probe. Maroon."

"Maroon." He wrote down this information. "Mileage?"

"One hundred and seventy thousand."

His frown got a little tighter. "Car that old, that many miles, most I can give you for it is five hundred dollars."

I blinked. Wasn't he even going to ask if it ran? I bit my lip, fighting a decidedly inconvenient attack of conscience.

Hector apparently mistook my silence for reluctance. "Six hundred. Most I can do. Take it or leave it."

I swallowed hard. "Where do I sign?"

I had never bought a car before. My father had purchased the first vehicle I'd driven, an orange Gremlin formerly owned by a dog trainer. Every time it rained, the car smelled of wet poodle. Steve bought the maroon Probe for me for Christmas one year. I'd wanted a blue Mustang, but he had surprised me with the Probe and I thought it would have appeared ungrateful to protest, though I could never look at the car without thinking of dental work.

"All right, then." Hector pushed back his chair and stood. "I'll show you what I've got in your price range."

For the next hour, I followed Hector around the lot as he showed me red Volkswagens, yellow Chevies and a lime-green car of indiscernible lineage. "Now darling, this is the perfect car for you," he said, patting the hood of the lime-green model. "Very sporty."

I stared at what looked to be an escapee from the bumper-car ride at the carnival. "I could never drive anything that color."

Hector took out an oversize handkerchief and mopped his forehead. "Well, honey, I wouldn't say in your price range you can afford to be picky. Besides—" he patted the car again

"—it's proven that cars this color are in fewer wrecks. Why do you think they paint fire engines green these days?"

A flash of blue caught my attention. That's when I saw it. My dream car. "What about that one?" I pointed toward a blue Mustang at the back corner of the lot.

"That one?" Hector rubbed his chin. "Yeah, I forgot about that one." He straightened. "Sure. I could make you a deal."

We walked over to the Mustang. It had a dent in one door and tired-looking upholstery. I slid into the driver's seat and turned the key. The engine coughed, then turned over. "Honey, I'd say it's you." Hector leaned in the window and grinned.

An hour later, I drove off the lot in the Mustang. I didn't really care that it was a ninety-six model or that it had a bumper sticker that read Onward Through the Fog. The important thing was that it was blue, the color of the dream car I'd never gotten. I'd taken it as a sign. I was on my own now, calling all the shots. And, by God, I was going to have that blue Mustang—my dream—dents and all.

THERE ARE TIMES WHEN I CONSIDER not having been born with pots of money to be a gross injustice. Just inside the door of the employee lounge at the Central Care Network Clinic where I work is a banner that proclaims: Two Million in Profits and Climbing! Whenever I see this, I feel majorly annoyed. Not only had I not been born with money, I had managed to find a job that guaranteed I wouldn't be getting my share of that two mil. Next to nurses' aides and janitors, transcriptionists are at the bottom of the hospital hierarchy.

But hey, I was young and single and had a new car, so what did I have to complain about, right? *Yeah, right,* I thought, as I boarded the elevator heading up to my cubicle in the family-practice section of the clinic the next day. I pasted a fake smile on my face as I entered the elevator. My mother had always told me I should smile even when I didn't feel like smiling because it would help me to develop the "habit of happiness." I preferred to think a permanent smile gave people doubts about your sanity, and thus they left you alone.

Family Practice was on the eleventh floor of the steel-and-glass high-rise in the Texas Medical Center complex. At every floor, the elevator doors parted and more people poured in as others exited. I found myself pushed farther and farther toward the rear of the car, until my nose was practically buried in the shellacked updo of an orthopedics receptionist.

I always got nervous when the elevator was this full. What if there was too much weight for the cables? What if it stopped between floors? Would we suffocate? Just last week Mary Joe Wisnewski from pediatrics had been stuck between floors for an hour.

And here I was, packed in like a teenager at dollar-a-car night at the drive-in. Two drug pushers—also known as pharmaceutical salesmen—hemmed me in on either side. I couldn't even move my arms.

So, of course, I had an itch I needed to scratch. On my butt. I shifted from one foot to the other, trying to ignore the persistent tickle on my right cheek as the elevator ground to a halt to take on still more passengers.

The tickle developed into a pinch. The hair on the back of my neck stood at attention as I realized the reason for my posterior disturbance. Some guy had his hand up my dress! He was poking and prodding my cheek like a baker testing dough. Or maybe he was a plastic surgeon who thought I was a likely candidate for a buttocks-lift.

I shifted, trying to move away from him, but in the packed elevator, it was impossible. The invisible groper started working on my other cheek. "Stop that!" I yelped.

My fellow passengers regarded me curiously, and there was a decided leaning away from me. Fury choked me.

Where did this pervert get off feeling me up like that? I'd show him.

I shifted my weight to my left leg and swung my right foot back, connecting solidly with the joker's kneecap. If I'd had more room, I would have aimed higher. As it was, he grunted and let me go. The doors opened and I surged forward, elbowing two old women out of the way as I broke for freedom.

I stood beside a potted palm in the corridor and tried to see into the elevator, to identify the man who'd groped me. But the doors shut before I could make out anyone. Sighing, I adjusted my purse on my shoulder and headed for the stairs to hike up the three floors to Family Practice.

"Phoebe, you're late." The office manager, Joan Lee, shoved a stack of patient folders into my hands. "Dr. Patterson is in rare form this morning." Standing four foot eleven inches in a size-one Jones New York suit, Joan looked like a geisha who'd gotten lost on her way to Wall Street. Her voice was soft as silk, but her backbone was diamond-hard steel. Insurance companies quaked at the sound of her name, and even the most bullheaded surgeon addressed her respectfully as "Ms. Lee, ma'am."

"He wants those charts on his desk by noon," Joan continued. "So you'd better get busy."

"No problem." I shifted the folders to my left arm and headed for the coffee machine for a fortifying cup. "Barb and I will split them up and have them done by eleven."

"Sorry, but Barb can't help you. I had to put her on the front desk this morning."

I turned, empty cup in hand. "Why? Where's Kathleen?"

Joan shook her head and disappeared around the corner. Dr. Patterson's nurse, Michelle, joined me at the coffee machine. "Kathleen was dismissed," she whispered as she spooned creamer into her cup.

I raised my eyebrows. "Turned him down again, did she?"

Dr. Patterson had been badgering the receptionist to go out with him for weeks now —despite the fact that both of them were married, and not to each other.

Michelle shrugged. "I guess so. Or maybe he decided to move on to greener pastures and didn't want her hanging around."

"Michelle, the doctor needs you in room three." Joan hurried past us, dragging a loaded lab cart. "Phoebe, don't forget those charts have to be done by noon."

"I can do it if the system cooperates. When is the new transcription system supposed to be installed?" I called after Joan's retreating back.

"Soon. You'll have to make do until then." She disappeared around the corner, test tubes rattling in her wake.

I headed for my workroom at the back of the office suite. Windowless and cramped, it resembled the supply closet it had once been. A long counter had been installed to hold the two computers and transcription equipment, and a single filing cabinet provided a place to stash my purse. Nothing fancy, but it was quiet, out of the flow of traffic and no one cared how many empty coffee cups or Diet Coke cans I let pile up as long as I got my work done on time.

I booted up my computer and popped the first tape into the transcription machine. Dr. Patterson's Texas twang filled my headphones. "The patient is a well-developed young woman of sixteen, presenting with pain in the left patella." I rolled my eyes as I typed. Patterson was always going on about the beauty or physical developments of his female patients. If they were over twenty-one he'd note if they were married or single and if they had any children. I wondered if he was making notes to himself for future reference.

I busted butt and finished the last of the tapes at ten after twelve and was fastening a printout onto the front of a patient chart when the intercom buzzed. "Doctor Patterson would like to see you in his office," Joan announced.

I groaned. What was he going to do, chew me out for being ten minutes late? "If he didn't go on so much about how big a patient's boobs or behind were, he'd shave half an hour off my transcription time," I muttered as I gathered up the charts and headed for the doctor's lair at the other end of the office.

Dr. Ken Patterson was a tall man with the broad shoulders and thick neck of a former football player. He, in fact, had been a linebacker for the University of Texas before deciding on a career in medicine. His hairline had receded in twin widow's peaks, frosted with gray, which only added to his distinguished good looks. Patients talked about how charming he was, but I thought there was more smarm than charm in the good doctor.

"Here are the charts you wanted." I deposited the stack of file folders on the corner of his desk. It was a massive mahogany piece that was big enough for a grown man to stretch out on. Rumor had it that Patterson had made good use of that space with more than one woman. Frankly, I was glad it wasn't my job to polish the thing. I turned to leave, but Patterson caught me by the arm.

"What's your hurry?" Still clutching my arm, he reached back and pushed the door closed.

I frowned. I didn't want to end up like Kathleen, with bills to pay and no job, but neither did I want to end up as Patterson's next plaything. "I have a lot of work to do," I said, trying to pull away from him.

"Yes, I've noticed how tense you've been lately." He released me, but continued to block my path to the door. "I think maybe you've been working too hard."

"I'm fine, really." I tried to dodge past him and collided with Albert, the life-size skeletal model grinning cheerfully from his stand next to the desk.

Albert clanked and swayed like a macabre set of wind chimes. At Halloween we dressed him up and stationed him by the reception desk with a bowl of candy, but the rest of the year Albert was a mute observer of the goings-on in Patterson's office. If those bones could talk...

"The real reason I wanted to see you is I have a question about one of the notes you transcribed for me." Patterson walked around the desk, seemingly all business, but I didn't let down my guard. He pulled a folder from a stack in his out box and beckoned me toward him. "It's right here. Please take a look and tell me what you think this means."

I leaned over the desk, staying as far from Patterson's octopus arms as possible. Fortunately, I could read upside down. "Patient is recently divorced, suffering from nervous strain." I looked up at Patterson. "I'm certain that's what you said on the tape. Is there something wrong?"

"Not wrong, but I couldn't help thinking how well that phrase describes your own situation." He pressed the tips of his fingers together and looked down his nose at me, as if I'd suddenly developed a rare disease. Or a third breast. "You know, Phoebe, not only am I your employer, but I think of myself as your physician, as well. It's obvious to me that since your divorce, you, too, have been exhibiting signs of nervous strain. I believe I can help you."

I started backing toward the door. "Dr. Michaels over at County General is my doctor."

For a man of his size, Patterson was amazingly quick. He came around the desk and pulled me to him in a bear hug. It was like being caught in the elevator doors, my ribs creaking, my breath cut off. "I find you so attractive," he murmured, and began kissing my neck. Wet slobbery kisses. You'd think a man who considered himself a modern-day Don Juan would have a better technique. I struggled, caught tight in his crazed grip.

Nose buried in my neck, his ear brushed up against my lips, pink and vulnerable. I know how to take advantage of a good opportunity when I see it. I bit down hard.

He screamed like a woman, a high-pitched shriek that was probably heard two floors away. I shot out of his arms and was standing by the door by the time he straightened up. He had one hand clapped over his ear and his eyes were wet. "Why did you do that?" he asked, seeming genuinely puzzled.

"Did I mention I have this thing about being held against my will?" I turned the doorknob. "I'm going to pretend this never happened," I said. "But if you so much as lay a hand on me again I'll report you to the AMA, the TMA, the BBB and anybody else who'll listen."

"Phoebe, Phoebe, Phoebe." He started toward me again, arms outstretched, pleading. "I know you've been without a man for months now. Surely you must need the physical release—"

I was out the door before he finished the sentence. My feet pounded down the carpeted hallway in time with my furiously beating heart. "What I need is to be left the hell alone," I muttered as I rounded the corner, headed toward the front office. Joan was going to hear about the doctor's latest shenanigans.

I didn't see the man at the end of the hallway until it was too late. I had a fleeting impression of broad shoulders and dark hair before I barreled into him. Papers scattered as he was shoved back against one wall. He struggled for balance, holding on to the only support available—me.

2

"GET YOUR HANDS OFF OF ME!" I swatted at the stranger as his fingers clutched at my dress.

"You're the one who ran into me, lady." He righted himself and stared down at me. He was quite tall and, in a better mood, I probably would have thought he was handsome, with his tousled dark hair and heavy-lidded eyes. He was fairly young, midtwenties, I guessed.

"You should watch where you're going," I snapped.

"I could say the same to you."

We glared at each other, both rumpled and out of breath. Not unlike two people in the aftermath of a particularly vigorous round of sex. I swallowed. Now why had I thought of that? Except, of course, that he was a particularly handsome man, and those dark eyes of his seemed to look right through me, as if he could tell I was wearing my best Givenchy underwear.

Stop it! I ordered myself. I glanced around, hoping someone would come to my rescue. The office was eerily silent and I realized everyone else had gone to lunch. Me and handsome Hank here were alone, except, of course, for the lecherous doctor.

I smoothed my hands down my sides. The thing to do was to stay calm and collected. That was me. Ms. Cool. "If you're here to see the doctor, his office is back there." I pointed down the hallway.

"Actually, I'm looking for a Phoebe Frame." The man

glanced around us. "Maybe you could point me in the right direction and I promise to stay out of your way."

"Phoebe Frame?" I felt my face warm. "Uh, what do you want with her?"

"Not that it's your business, but I'm here to install a new transcription system. She is the transcriptionist, isn't she?"

"Yes." The word came out as a squeak. I straightened and tried to look indifferent. "I'm Phoebe. If you'll follow me, the transcription room is right this way."

I marched past him, down the hall toward my cubicle. By now it felt as if my whole face and neck were on fire. And red is not my best color. Not that I cared what handsome Hank thought of my looks, but...

I stopped at the doorway to my cubicle and whirled to face him. "You haven't told me your name."

"You didn't give me time." He offered me a card. "Jeff Fischer. My friends call me Jeff, but you can call me Mr. Fischer."

All right, maybe I deserved that. I cleared my throat. "Look, I'm sorry about, well, about just now. I was very annoyed at someone and you were in the wrong place at the wrong time."

He set his briefcase on the counter and opened it. "Yeah, well, I guess you weren't hired for your personality anyway, huh?"

"I said I was sorry."

"Forget about it."

"Oh, that is so like a man."

"What are you talking about?"

"You insult me, and then you try to blow it off as if it isn't important."

"Hey, you insulted me first."

"I did not."

"Yes, you did. You accused me of trying to grope you when I was only trying to keep my balance."

"You *were* groping me." I flushed, remembering the feel of his hand on my breast. "Though I'll admit, you probably didn't do it on purpose."

He looked up at the ceiling, addressing some invisible being. "She admits she's wrong. That must be a first."

"How can you say that? You don't even know me."

He grinned. "No, but I'd like to." He stuck out his hand. "Let's start over. I'm Jeff Fischer. Nice to meet you, Miss Frame. Or is it Mrs.?"

"It's Ms." I shook his hand, ignoring the flutter in my stomach at his touch. Maybe I was just hungry. "Nice to meet you, too, Mr. Fischer."

"I thought we were going to be friends now. Call me Jeff."

"All right, Jeff. I'll, uh, just leave you to your work."

"Sure you don't want to stick around? You could tell me what I'm doing wrong."

"No, I think I'll go to lunch." I backed toward the door. With any luck, Jeff wouldn't be here when I got back. The last thing I needed right now was a young, handsome man with a sarcastic sense of humor.

Or maybe it was the *first* thing I needed. Sometimes the two extremes aren't that far apart.

ON THURSDAYS, I ALWAYS HAVE LUNCH with my friend Darla. After the morning I'd had, I figured our lunch would be the one spot of sanity in my day. A tall blonde with an Ivana Trump updo, Darla is not only my best gal pal and chief partner-in-crime, she's also my hairdresser—the only person who knows my real hair color—and the keeper of all my secrets.

"You got new wheels!" she squealed as I pulled to the curb in front of Hair Apparent, the salon where she works. She climbed into the passenger seat. "What happened to your old ride?" She flipped down the passenger side visor and fluffed her bangs in the makeup mirror.

"The Probe died yesterday afternoon, smoke pouring out from under the hood and everything."

"So you just walked down the street and bought a new one?" Darla's perfectly plucked eyebrows rose in amazement.

I shrugged. "It was either that, or call a taxi."

I turned into the lot of Taco Loco and found a parking place. Darla followed me inside and we slid into our usual booth. "I never knew anyone who decided to buy a car and just did it," she said. "I mean, aren't you supposed to research these things? Take test-drives?"

The waitress set two glasses of iced tea and a basket of hot chips in front of us. "The usual?" she asked.

"The usual," we chorused. Chicken chalupas with guacamole. Best in the city. I turned back to Darla. "That's how Steve bought cars. How my father bought cars." In fact, it was how every man I knew bought cars. Did that make it right?

Darla raised her glass in a toast. "To Phoebe's new wheels," she said. "May they take you places you've always wanted to go."

I liked the sound of that, even if I had yet to figure out where it was I was headed. "What's new with you?" I asked.

She suddenly became very interested in the placemat in front of her, eyes avoiding mine. "Well..." She pursed her lips. "I heard some news today. Something I don't think you'll especially enjoy hearing."

I sipped my tea and tried not to look too interested. News meant gossip and it felt unseemly to appear overeager to indulge in something that, after all, was supposed to be a vice. "News about what?" I asked after a moment.

"News about Steve and Miss Just-a-waitress."

Darla's nose for news had discovered that the teenybopper

Steve had started dating three months into his midlife search for "happiness" worked at the Yellow Rose, one of those cabaret places euphemistically known as gentlemen's clubs. The girl—Tami—swore she was "just a waitress," though from what I had seen, she was certainly well qualified to wear tassels, or whatever sort of excuse for a costume was customary for dancers in those places. "I don't want to hear it," I said, and shut my mouth firmly, as if to hold back any sign of the curiosity that was already spreading over me like a rash.

"You're going to find out sooner or later." She leaned across the table, her voice soft. "And I think it's something you'd much prefer to hear from me."

My stomach quivered. I hated this—hated caring what Steve and his girlfriend were up to. My goal in life was not to care, to be serene and happy and above it all.

But I wasn't there yet. I took another swallow of tea, trying to wet my too-dry mouth. "What is it?"

Darla studied her perfect manicure. "Just-a-waitress came into the shop today."

I waited, but apparently Darla required some sort of reaction before proceeding. "Did she have an appointment, or just drop by to say hi?"

"She had an appointment. With Henry." She made a face. "Good thing it wasn't with me, or she'd have walked out bald."

I held back a snicker. Tami had gorgeous long blond hair. The idea of her without that crowning glory had a certain nasty appeal. "So what's the scoop? Did she get dreadlocks, or a pierced nose?"

Darla shook her head. "Didn't you say Steve never wanted children?"

There went my stomach again, acting as if I'd just plunged five stories in the front car of a roller coaster. "Yes. I mean, no, he never wanted children. He said they would make things too complicated."

I put a hand over my belly, not even realizing until it was too late that I'd done so. In the early days, I'd thought I'd change Steve's mind, that one day we'd have a family. Even as recently as last year, I'd been telling myself we had plenty of time. "What are you saying, Darla?"

"I'm saying Steve's life is about to get pretty complicated. Just-a-waitress is four or five months gone."

I counted back in my head. That meant it had happened after our divorce six months ago. We'd been separated six months before that. Plenty of time for me to get over the guy, right? Why should I care what he and his girlfriend were up to?

"You don't look so good." Darla leaned forward and studied my face,

"I'll be okay in a minute," I managed to squeak out.

"Okay is a relative term." She frowned. "You want to talk about it?"

I shook my head. No, I wasn't okay. And no, I didn't want to talk about it.

The waitress brought our food and I focused on adding salsa to my chalupa, glad of an excuse not to say anything. Even if I'd wanted to spill my guts to Darla, I didn't think I could have found the words to describe how I felt.

Something ugly and black had attached itself to my insides, some slimy emotional specter that was, in turns, angry and disgusted. I'd put off having children because Steve didn't want them, yet our divorce papers were scarcely cold before he knocked up some other woman. Outside, I was mute, lips welded together by pride. But inside, I was screaming.

"So, what are you going to do now?" Darla scooped guacamole onto a chip and popped it into her mouth.

Last I heard, murder was still illegal. I sighed and laid aside my empty spoon. "What can I do? I have to get on with my life."

She eyed me critically. "Starting when? It's been six months since the divorce and almost a year since Steve walked out. Have you been on a single date?"

"Just what I need—another man in my life." I shook my head. "No, thank you."

"They aren't all bad. You like Tony, don't you?"

Tony was a truck driver Darla referred to as her rustproof lover—"heart of gold and buns of steel." He was also a genuinely sweet guy. "You got the last good one," I said.

"Oh, come on. You're still young. Attractive. You could find someone nice."

I shook my head. "Who would I date? In my job all the men I meet are either old, sick or married." The image of a certain studly computer installer popped up to call me a liar. Okay, so Jeff Fischer was gorgeous and I hadn't noticed a ring on his hand. He was also young and sarcastic and I hadn't exactly wowed him with my charm. "I don't need another man in my life," I said, stabbing a fork into my chalupa for emphasis.

"Just think about it," Darla said gently.

I nodded. "I'll think about it." But thinking and doing are two entirely different animals, aren't they?

I RETURNED TO WORK AFTER LUNCH and discovered the cubbyhole had been ransacked. My computer processor sat in the hall, my transcription machine balanced atop it. My monitor occupied my chair and half a mile of cable coiled around the doorway like so many snakes prepared to wrap around my ankles.

I picked my way through this maze and stepped into the room, only to be confronted with one of the finest specimens of male *gluteus maximus* I've ever been privileged to see.

The butt in question wasn't naked, more's the pity, but the

expertly tailored slacks molded around it did a nice job of showing it to advantage.

"What are you staring at?" The rest of the man in question emerged from beneath my desk.

"Jeff! Uh, hello." I moved over and pretended to be interested in a stack of computer manuals. "Was I staring?"

He pointed a screwdriver at me. "You were staring. And smiling."

"I'm just delighted at the prospect of finally getting the new transcription system installed." I kept my eyes on the manual, pretending to be reading, but I was really trying to identify the cologne he was wearing. Something spicy, faintly exotic...

"I didn't know you read Chinese." He'd risen and was looking over my shoulder.

I glanced down at the booklet in my hand. Rows of Chinese characters danced across the page. I snapped the booklet shut. "I was studying the diagrams." I pointed to the snarl of cables streaming out from under my desk. "Don't you think you should do something about all that?"

"Your usual sunny self, I see." He kneeled and began fiddling with something under my desk. "And here I thought we were going to be friends."

I didn't want to be friends with Jeff Fischer. He was too young, too good-looking, too full of himself, too *male.* Men were not at the top of my list these days. I kicked at the tangle of cables. "How am I supposed to get any work done with everything scattered all over the place like this?"

"I'll have it all back together in no time." His head disappeared beneath the desk once more.

"With this new system, you'll be faster than ever." He reached up and patted the desktop. "Have a seat and keep me company."

I backed toward the door. "Maybe I'd better leave you alone to do your work."

"I work better when I have a pretty woman to talk to."

I resented the flutter that ran through my stomach. As if a compliment from a smart-ass like him meant anything. I told myself I was only staying because if I went back up front Joan would put me to work labeling urine samples, or filing test results or some equally odious chore.

So I took a seat on the desk, next to a canvas satchel that spilled tools across the desktop. It wasn't the most comfortable position. My feet didn't touch the ground, which left my legs swinging practically in Jeff's face. Why had I decided this was a good day to wear my chartreuse-with-white-polka-dots slip dress?

"That's better." Jeff's gaze traveled from my exposed knees to my ankles. "Very nice."

He grinned in a way that might have been lecherous on someone who didn't already look like an Eagle Scout. "How old are you?" I blurted.

He arched one eyebrow. "Old enough to know my way around."

"No really. How old?"

"I'm twenty-six." He said it as if he was announcing a winning Lotto number. "How old are you?"

"Too old for you." I inched farther away from him.

"I prefer experienced women." He went back to operating his screwdriver.

Experienced? Was that anything like a used car being "experienced"? Or did I look like a woman who'd been around the block a few times? "What makes you think I'm experienced?"

"Let's just say you don't strike me as a recent escapee from a convent."

"Someone told you I was divorced. That Michelle—"

"No, I didn't know that. I was thinking more about the hickey on your neck."

I clapped my hand to my neck so hard the skin stung. Heat washed over me and I knew my face was bright red. "I do not have a hickey!" Where would I have gotten one? I hadn't been intimate with a man since.... A sick feeling washed over me as I recalled my prelunch wrestling session with Dr. P. The bastard.

Jeff stood and dropped the screwdriver into the tool bag. "It's not that noticeable," he said. "It's just above your collar, right...there." His finger brushed across my skin, a feather touch that made every nerve ending vibrate with awareness. I took a deep breath, trying to regain my composure, but all that did was draw his spicy, exotic, masculine scent into my lungs. I stared at the V of naked chest showing in the open throat of his shirt and fought the insane urge to plant a kiss right...there.

Hormones. That had to be it. They were like ants. They'd been fine, not bothering me at all in the year since Steve had called it quits. Content to go about the business of doing whatever hormones were supposed to do in the body. And then the stud here had disturbed them. One touch from him and the hormones had come to life like an anthill stirred with a stick. And they apparently weren't going to calm down anytime soon. I wouldn't be safe around any being with a hint of testosterone. The next thing I knew, I'd be leering at old men in elevators and flirting with the teenager behind the counter at McDonald's.

"I have to go." I slid off the desk, scattering three screwdrivers and a socket set in my hurry to escape.

I fled to the ladies' room and contemplated my red face in the mirror. Wincing, I pulled back my hair and studied the purpling love bite. "That no-good Dr. Lech. I ought to—"

"Phoebe, hurry up in there." Michelle pounded on the door. "I have to go."

I grabbed my purse and groped through it, in vain hope I'd find a scarf to cover the evidence of a definite lapse in judgment. But I didn't wear scarves. I searched the supply cabinet mounted over the toilet. Nothing but half a box of tampons, two cans of hair spray, six rolls of toilet paper and a pink toothbrush. Short of wrapping toilet paper around my neck, I was stuck.

I opened the door and sidled past Michelle, my head down so that my hair fell forward to cover the side of my neck. "Are you okay?" she asked.

"I'm fine. Do we have any bandages?"

"Sure. In the lab. Over the sink. Did you cut yourself?"

"Just a paper cut," I mumbled, and hurried to the lab.

I was studying my reflection in the paper-towel dispenser, making sure I'd covered the mark, when Michelle came into the lab. "You got a paper cut on your neck?"

I straightened and tugged my collar a little higher. "I, uh, was carrying some charts and one slipped." Was I a pathetic liar, or what?

Michelle laughed. "Reminds me of high school. We used to put Band-Aids over hickeys. As if everyone didn't know what was under there." She picked up the blood-draw tray and turned to leave, but paused in the doorway. "You'd better watch those paper cuts, Phoebe. A girl can't be too careful, you know."

She giggled and left the room. I sagged against the counter. Great. Now the whole office would think I'd been up to something. If only I *had* been up to something. At least I'd have great memories to go along with the hickey.

The staccato tap of high heels on linoleum announced Joan Lee's approach. "What are you doing hiding in here?" she asked. She peered closer. "What is that on your neck?"

"Vampire. Met him in the park last night. I'm thinking maybe I ought to go home in case I suddenly develop a desire to start biting people."

Joan frowned. "There are no such things as vampires. Besides, you can't go home. Dr. Patterson wants to see you."

"Speaking of bloodsuckers..."

Joan frowned. "He's in his office. Don't keep him waiting. He has patients to see."

When Joan heard humor was contagious, she was the first in line to be immunized against it.

3

RELUCTANTLY, I MADE MY WAY to Dr. Patterson's office.

Albert grinned at me from his usual post. Someone had crowned him with a Houston Astros ball cap. "Orange is not your color," I told him. "It does nothing for your complexion."

"Good afternoon, Phoebe." Dr. Patterson looked up from a patient chart. "Did you have a pleasant lunch?" He frowned. "What's wrong with your neck?"

"You're what's wrong with it." I glared at him. "When you groped me earlier, you gave me a hickey."

He blinked, his expression bland. "Obviously, you're delusional." He consulted the papers in his hand, suddenly all business. "I'd like you to help me with some research I'm doing for my upcoming presentation at the annual Texas Medical Association conference. It's a tremendous honor to be selected and my presentation must be perfect."

Right. This was all about him. What else was new? "I'm a transcriptionist," I said, trying to match his chilly demeanor. "I don't see how I could help—"

"I'd ask the receptionist to take care of it, but until we hire a new one, that position is vacant and I can't wait to prepare this presentation." He handed me a sheet torn from a yellow legal pad. "Besides, you're not busy right now, not with the new transcription system being installed. All you have to do is conduct a Web search for the topics listed here."

I frowned at the list of medical terms on the paper. "I'm not sure what these mean."

"You're welcome to use my reference books to look up anything you need." He nodded toward an oak bookcase against the far wall. "And I'll be happy to assist you when I have the time." His smile was just short of a leer.

I folded the sheet of paper. "Would this assignment involve working late?" *With you?*

He moved toward me. "I promise you'll be rewarded."

I prepared to dodge out of the way when Joan Lee appeared in the doorway, trailed by a drug pusher in a gray suit. You hang around doctors' offices long enough, you can spot these guys and gals. Expensive suits, perfectly styled hair, imported sports cars—everything about them screams big bucks, including their perfectly straight, gleaming white teeth. Those teeth were always on display as they grinned and glad-handed their way through the office. They passed out pens and sticky notes like candy. Sometimes they even passed out candy. At Christmas, they brought elaborate gift baskets, which the doctor usually kept for himself.

I didn't intend to let this interruption derail our discussion. With any luck, the pusher would be in and out in a few minutes and I could tell Patterson exactly what he could do with his little extra "project."

I drifted to the bookcase and pretended to be interested in the *Merck Manual.*

"I brought those samples you asked about, doc." The salesman's voice boomed through the office as he opened his sample case.

Patterson glanced at me, but I kept turning pages in the big green book, feigning avid interest in a description of contact dermatitis.

"Great, Jerry. Thanks a lot."

Jerry pulled out a cardboard tray of little boxes. Each bottle would contain a few pills of medication, meant to be handed out as samples to patients, who would then be convinced enough of the drug's benefits to opt for a full prescription. "Everything they say about this stuff is true," Jerry gushed. "It'll sure put pep in your pecker."

By now I had a pretty good idea of what drug Jerry was peddling. Sure enough, every box in that tray was emblazoned with the familiar blue tablet and a capital *V*.

To my secret delight, a stain of red crept up the back of Patterson's neck. He hastily shoved the samples in his desk and ushered Jerry from the room.

As soon as they were gone, I replaced the *Merck* on the shelf and rushed to the desk. I opened the drawer and took out the tray of little boxes. Sure enough, it was Viagra. As if the doc needed any more pep in his pecker.

I didn't have time to open all the little boxes and empty each bottle, so I dropped the whole tray in the trash can beside Patterson's desk and carried it out with me.

I passed Joan in the hall and she gave me a curious look.

"I thought since I wasn't busy, I'd try to clean up a little around here," I said.

At the end of the hall, I ducked into the ladies' room and emptied every bottle in the toilet. Then I stuffed Patterson's trash can in the supply closet and sauntered back into the corridor, humming to myself. My bad mood had vanished. I felt almost giddy. I didn't know what had come over me. I'd never done anything so daring in my life.

I pushed aside a momentary nudge of guilt by telling myself that Patterson deserved this small payback after the way he'd treated me. Women everywhere would be thankful if they knew what I'd just done.

I passed Jeff near the end of the hallway. "What are you looking so smug about?" he asked.

I gave him what I hoped was a mysterious smile. "My

mama always said nothing would make your day like doing a good deed for someone else and she was right."

He angled himself against the wall, blocking my way. "What good deed did you do?"

I shook my finger at him. "Oh, but it's more virtuous to do your good deeds in secret."

"Since when are you virtuous?" He reached out and stroked the bandage at my throat. "Barney. Definitely your style."

I fought against a blush. "It was all we had. They're very popular with kids. Would you like one?"

His voice was a low rumble that set up vibrations in my chest. "I can think of a few things I'd like from you, but a Band-Aid isn't one of them."

My knees suddenly felt wobbly. I fought the urge to hold on to him for support. "Dream on," I said, sounding a little out of breath.

He leaned closer, a decidedly wicked grin making him more handsome than ever. "Sometimes dreams come true, you know."

He let me by him and I tottered to my room, which was miraculously back together. A mixture of victorious exaltation and frustrated desire made me giddy. So Jeff wasn't right for me? A woman could flirt, couldn't she? I probably needed the practice. And putting one over on "Dr. Love" was enough to make anyone happy.

I sank into my chair. Yes, from now on I wasn't putting up with crap from anybody. I was declaring a one-woman revolution. I reached for the phone and punched in Darla's number.

"Darla, I want to make an appointment. I need a color job."

"Okay. Let me make sure I have some Bashful Blonde in stock."

I glanced at my reflection in the darkened computer monitor. "Forget the blond. I'm ready for a change."

"A change? What kind of a change?" She sounded alarmed.

I twirled a lock of hair around my finger. "I think I'm ready for something more exciting. More daring." My grin widened. "I'm ready to be a redhead."

AT FIVE O'CLOCK ON THE DOT, I escaped from work, leaving Jeff on his hands and knees in my office, threading computer wire along the baseboards. "Leaving already?" he asked as I walked past.

"I have an important appointment."

"Another hot date with the vampire?" He had a way of arching one eyebrow when he said something meant to tease me that made my mouth go dry.

Hormones, I reminded myself. *Just those damned hormones.* "Next time I see him, I'll drive a stake through his heart."

Jeff put a hand over his heart. "Remind me to never rub you the wrong way."

You're never going to rub me the right way, either, I thought, but did my best to keep the sentiment from my face. Jeff Fischer was sexier than any man had a right to be, but he was also six years younger than me. Not that much older than Just-a-waitress. Wouldn't Steve laugh if he thought I was having my own midlife crisis?

With that thought souring my mood, I drove to Hair Apparent. It was one of those huge places with six stylists, two manicurists, a tanning booth and a massage therapist. The year before, they'd added the words Day Spa to their name and prices had shot up twenty percent. But I stayed with the place because of Darla. It's hard enough to find a friend these days, and even harder to find a good hair stylist.

Darla greeted me with what looked like a giant, economy-size bottle of ketchup in her hand. "What do you think?" she asked, holding up the bottle so that a beam of sunlight from the front window struck it. "It's called Ravishing Ruby."

"It looks like ketchup." Maybe my decision to be a redhead had been a little hasty....

"It looks better on. Trust me." She shoved me into a chair and wrapped me in a plastic cape.

"What's with the Barney bandage on your neck?" she asked as she fastened the cape.

"You don't want to know." I grabbed a magazine off the counter beside the chair and opened it at random.

"There are two people you do not keep secrets from in this world—your hairdresser and your best friend. I happen to be both, so spill."

I didn't have to look in the mirror to know my face was redder than my hair was going to be. "I had a run-in with Dr. P. this morning. Apparently, he's got the idea that I should be his next conquest."

She frowned. "The lech. But what does that have to do with the bandage on your neck?"

"He, uh, apparently thought it would be cute to leave his mark on me," I said grimly.

"No! A hickey?" Darla's squeal silenced every other conversation in the room. Chairs swiveled in our direction and the other stylists froze, combs and scissors poised as they waited for the next revelation.

I sank down in the chair. Darla began combing out sections of hair and everyone else went back to work. "That man's got a lot of nerve. You ought to report him."

"Yeah, like that hasn't been tried before. It never does any good. He's this big respected doctor and I'm just some sex-starved receptionist." I frowned at my reflection in the salon mirror. "No, the best thing to do is to just stay out of his way until he gets tired of it and decides to pick on somebody else."

Darla's scowl let me know what she thought of that strategy, but a good friend knows when to keep her mouth shut. She shook the ketchup bottle and began squirting color onto my hair. I closed my eyes. It looked like the fake blood they used in movies. I could always tell people I'd been the victim of a tragic accident.

"What did people at work say?" she asked.

"Most of them didn't notice. The only one who gave me a hard time about it was Jeff."

"Jeff? Who's Jeff?"

I opened my eyes. "This kid who's installing my new transcription equipment."

"Just how old is this kid? And is he good-looking?"

I shifted in the chair. "Too young. Twenty-six."

"Oooh. Twenty-six is a good age in men. They're too old for fraternity parties and most of them still have all their hair. He's handsome, I'll bet. He must be, or you wouldn't have ignored the question."

I picked a piece of lint off the cape. "I wouldn't call him ugly." Tall, muscular, thick brown hair, dark brown eyes—no, that definitely wasn't my idea of ugly. "It doesn't matter what he looks like."

"He's that good, huh? So, are you gonna go out with him?"

"I'm not going out with him. He's just a kid." I swiveled the chair around so suddenly Darla missed my head altogether and a big blob of the fake-blood-looking hair color landed on my shoulder and dripped down the front of the cape.

Darla wiped at the spilled color with an old towel. "Twenty-six is not a kid. And he's only six years younger than you. Just because you married an old man when you were nineteen doesn't make *you* old. Besides, haven't you heard that younger men and older women are more compatible sexually? There was a therapist on *Oprah* last week talking about it."

Maybe six years didn't sound like much to most people, but it felt like more than six years to me. I was mature for my age. Though come to think of it, that doesn't sound like the compliment now that it did when I was nineteen. "Darla, he's installing some computer equipment in my office. There isn't anything sexual about that."

"Sure there's not." Her expression told me she didn't buy it. "He's just a hot young stud who is interested enough in you to notice a love bite from another man on your neck and comment on it. And you've just spent ten minutes protesting how impossible it would be for you to have the slightest interest in him. That's longer than you've talked about any man other than Steve the sleaze."

I glared at her in the mirror. She laughed. "All right, I'll drop the subject if you tell me one thing."

"What's that?" I was still suspicious. Darla had a way of getting confessions out of me that I didn't want to give.

"Did this Jeff guy have anything to do with your sudden decision to become a redhead?" She pointed at my reflection in the mirror. "And be honest."

"It didn't have anything to do with Jeff." I smoothed the cape across my lap. "I've thought about this for years."

"Then why didn't you do it before?"

"Steve wouldn't let me." Even as I said the words, I knew they sounded pathetic.

"What did he do, lock you in the house and threaten to take away your car keys?" She shook her head and made clucking noises under her tongue. "Sorry. I just can't stand it when men try to tell their wives what they can't do with their hair or their clothes or anything like that. It's like they think women are children who need to be kept in line."

"Steve always told me he liked my hair just the way it

was," I said wistfully. In fact, the first thing he ever said to me was "Hey beautiful, do blondes really have more fun?"

Okay, so it wasn't a great pickup line. I was nineteen at the time. Steve was thirty and I thought he was suave and sophisticated. I didn't care what he said to me as long as he said *something*.

"Well, I'm glad you decided to do this." Darla set her minute timer and grinned at me. "It's going to look great. So why now? What happened to make you decide to do it today?

I managed a smile in return. "You might say I owe it all to some samples of Viagra."

"Viagra? The sex pill? Are they giving it to women now?"

"Nope. And a certain troublemaking man won't be taking it, either." I told her about swiping the doctor's samples and dumping them down the toilet. "It was sneaky," I concluded. "But it sure felt good."

"Sneaky? It was brilliant. And it serves him right, the old lecher."

"I'm sure he'll just get more samples, but it makes me feel like I have a little power over him now. I know his big secret."

"Speaking of secrets, I have some more news about your ex and Just-a-waitress."

I squirmed in the chair, remembering the last "news" Darla had told me. "I'm not sure I want to know."

"You're going to know soon enough, anyhow. When she was in here she also told Henry that she and Steve-o are getting married."

My stomach clenched and I locked my jaw, freezing my face into what I hoped was an indifferent expression. I shouldn't have been surprised, considering that they were going to have a baby, but the information hit me like a punch.

"Oh, hon." Darla put her hand on my shoulder. "You didn't really want him back, did you?"

I shook my head so hard little drops of color spattered

across the front of Darla's smock. "No. Never." I *didn't* want him back. But Steve marrying someone else was the final evidence that a chapter in my life was over. He was moving on, but what was I doing? I lived in the same house, held the same job, did the same things and I was still alone.

"Come on over here to the shampoo bowl." Darla nudged me toward the back of the shop. "If you like, I do a pretty good rendition of 'I'm Gonna Wash That Man Right Out of My Hair.'"

A bit of a smile broke through my gloom. "I don't think that's necessary."

She patted my shoulder. "You'll feel better once you see the new you. I guarantee a certain younger man is going to be hot for you once he sees you in red."

"It's been a long time since anyone was even lukewarm," I said. "I don't see why Jeff should be any different."

"But you want him to be, don't you?" She put her face close to mine, staring into my eyes. "Don't lie, Phoebe Elaine Frame."

I shrugged. "Sure, I'd be flattered if some gorgeous young stud thought I was all that. But it's not going to happen."

"It could."

"Even if it does, I don't think it would be smart to get involved with him."

She turned on the water and tested the temperature against her wrist. "Who said anything about smart? What you want at this point in your life is fun. You haven't had nearly enough of that lately. Sounds like young Jeff could be just the ticket."

One way or round trip? I wondered as warm water cascaded over my scalp. Or did it really matter? If I was only going along for a pleasure cruise, did it really matter where it took me or how long it lasted?

4

I HAD A HARD TIME KEEPING my eyes on the road on the way home that evening. I kept tilting my head to look in the rear-view mirror at the stranger who stared back at me. Oh, she had the eyes, mouth and nose I was used to seeing when I looked at my reflection, but she also had a gorgeous head of shiny, copper-colored hair. I smiled every time I saw this "other" me. Suddenly, my eyes were bluer, my skin looked creamier. And all because of a change in hair color. "Who would have thought?" I murmured, and forced my gaze back to the road. I couldn't wait to show off my new look at work tomorrow. What would Jeff say?

I smiled, imagining his reaction. I was still smiling when an ominous *clunk* sounded from beneath the hood, followed by a horrifying grinding noise. I put on my blinker and steered onto the shoulder. The grinding grew louder and I shut off the engine and stared out the front windshield. A bitter odor wafted up through the air-conditioning vents.

A string of choice curses fought to climb up my throat, but what came out of my mouth was "OhGodohGodohGod." I bailed out of the car and hurried to pop the hood. The acrid odor was stronger. Was it my imagination, or did the whole engine appear to be leaning to one side?

I backed away, eyeing the car warily. The urge to kick something was strong, but I'm superstitious about cars. I think they can sense when you're upset with them, and mechanical failure is their chief way to get back at you.

Yeah, I know people *say* cars can't think, but who says they don't have intuition? The minute you begin to hate one, they know it and will make your life miserable.

I stomped to the shoulder and looked out at the traffic flying past. Someone would stop soon and maybe they'd have a phone I could use to call a wrecker.

A pickup sped by so close its tires slung gravel at me. A chorus of catcalls and whistles sailed toward me.

Cars honked. Men whistled. One made an obscene gesture. Another man yelled that he was in love with me. Women looked the other way. Some even changed lanes so they wouldn't have to drive on my side of the road. But no one stopped.

So much for chivalry or Good Samaritans. I searched the shoulder for a good-size rock. The next idiot who made a rude suggestion was going to get it in the windshield.

I'd found what I thought was a good weapon when a black pickup slowed and pulled in behind me. "Thank God," I said, walking toward the truck. "I thought no one was going to st—"

The door opened and a pair of long legs in tan slacks emerged, followed by a pair of broad shoulders and strong arms. I swallowed and grinned weakly. "Hello, Jeff. Imagine meeting you here."

He took a long time looking at me, his gaze traveling from the tips of my pink-painted toenails to the top of my coppery hair. "I like it," he said at last. "Very sexy."

I wasn't sure if he meant my new hair color or me in general, but I didn't dare ask. "What do you know about cars?"

"A little."

I followed him around to my upraised hood. He looked at it for a moment, then leaned in and wiggled something. Then he slammed the hood. "Broken motor mount," he said.

"Is that expensive to fix?" Who was I kidding? Everything about cars is expensive to fix.

"Shouldn't be too bad. How long have you had the car?"

"I just got it yesterday."

"Then it should be under some kind of dealer warranty. I'd take it back to where you bought it." He slipped a phone from his shirt pocket. "We'll call a wrecker to tow it to the dealer."

"Won't they be closed?" It was almost seven.

"If it is, the wrecker driver can leave it in the yard and you can stop by tomorrow to arrange everything." He punched in a number. "What's the name of the dealer?"

"Easy Motors. Over on Alameda."

He made a face, then spoke to someone on the line. "Ben? This is Jeff Fischer. I've got a friend here who has a Mustang with a broken motor mount. Can you tow it for her to an Easy Motors, over on Alameda?"

He gave the driver directions, then disconnected. "He'll be here in ten minutes."

"Thanks." Now that the car was taken care of, it felt awkward standing here with him. Cars raced past, stirring up dust that blew back at us in a hot wind.

He took my arm and steered me toward his truck. "Let's wait inside."

The truck was clean and relatively new. It smelled of leather and Jeff's cologne. I sat on the edge of the seat, next to the door and found myself imagining what it would feel like to lie back in that cool leather seat, with Jeff slowly undressing me....

See what kind of trouble hormones will get you into? I crossed my arms and my legs and wondered if Jeff would think I was strange if I asked him to turn up the air conditioner. The air in that cab was definitely too warm.

"So, Red." He turned toward me, grinning. "Did I ever tell you I have a thing for redheads?"

My heart pounded. "Uh...what kind of thing?"

He slid his hand along the back of the seat, toward me. "I think they're very...exciting."

"Sorry to disappoint you, but I'm not an exciting person." But I was definitely getting excited. I squeezed my legs together and tucked my hair behind my ears. "So, did you finish installing the transcription system?"

His grin never faltered. "Don't think you're going to get rid of me that easily. I'm under contract to stick around and teach you how to use the new software."

I swallowed hard, imagining hours spent in my little cubicle with Mr. Testosterone. "I've been a transcriptionist for years. What's to learn?"

His eyes darkened and his voice lowered. "Oh, I'm betting I could teach you a lot."

He moved a little closer. I couldn't decide whether to scream or throw myself at him. Throwing myself at him was definitely winning out when a horn sounded behind us and a purple-and-black wrecker pulled alongside.

We climbed out of the truck and met the wrecker driver beside my car. He was a whip-thin man with long gray hair pulled back in a ponytail, his denim work shirt rolled up to reveal arms corded with muscle. "Hey, Jeff. How's your old man?"

"Doing great, Ben. Thanks for coming out. This is Phoebe Frame."

Ben nodded, then turned to the car. "You bought this from Easy Motors?"

I nodded. "I've only had it since yesterday, so it's still under warranty—isn't it?"

Ben made a noise that might have been laughter. "Good luck getting anything out of that bunch."

I retrieved my purse and Ben hooked the car up to

the wrecker. I started to climb in beside him, but Jeff pulled me back. "Ben can take care of it. I'll drive you home."

I didn't think that was a good idea, but before I could say anything, I heard clanking chains and tires on gravel and Ben pulled out into traffic, my Mustang hoisted behind him like the catch of the day.

"Okay. Thanks." At least driving, he'd have to keep his hands to himself. As for me, I could always sit on *my* hands.

"I'm starved. Let's get something to eat."

Eating was too much like a date. I was not going to date Jeff. "I really need to get home," I said.

"You have kids?"

The question jolted me. "Uh...no."

"Good."

Good? "Why is that good?" Was the world infested with men who didn't like children?

"It means you don't need to get home. And everybody has to eat, don't they?"

We ended up at a place called Pizza Junction, which combined Old West decor with Italian food in a sort of spaghetti Western theme. "You've eaten here before?" I asked as we made our way past bales of hay festooned with braids of garlic.

"It's very good." He slid into a booth and I sat across from him. "I recommend the Lariat Special."

I ordered a Diet Coke and agreed to split the Lariat Special with Jeff. He apparently wasn't a man who believed in small talk. As soon as the waitress brought our drinks, he looked me over and asked, "How long have you been divorced?"

I stripped the paper from a straw and wadded it into a knot, avoiding his gaze. "Six months. We were separated six months before that." Anticipating the next question, and wanting to get it over with, I added. "We were married twelve years."

"Was it your idea, or his?"

I had to hand it to Jeff; he had nerve. I imagined him tackling computer problems this way: find out everything you can so that you approach the problem armed with information. I could have told him these things were none of his business, but why bother? It wasn't as if I had any real secrets to hide. "It was his idea. He said he didn't want to be married anymore." I swished my straw around in my Diet Coke. "He has a young girlfriend now."

He took a long pull on his beer. "He's crazy."

"Because he left, or because he took up with a younger woman?"

"Both. What could a younger woman offer that you couldn't?"

He sounded so certain of right and wrong here. So naive. "You don't understand now, but one day you will. Of course, right now, younger women for you are in high school."

He leaned back against the booth. "I've always been partial to older women."

"Then go visit the nursing home."

He grinned. "Touchy, touchy. You know what I mean."

The arrival of our pizza saved me from having to find an answer to that. Jeff was telling me he was interested in me and I couldn't deny the powerful physical attraction I felt for him.

As we worked our way around the pizza, I turned the conversation to safer topics. I found out Jeff owned the company that distributed the software I was going to be using, as well as a number of other medical and dental programs. He had a small office with a few employees and spent most of his time in medical offices, selling or setting up new systems.

"Is every office as much of a soap opera as ours?" I asked.

"Pretty much." He looked thoughtful. "They're mostly

women, you know, so it's always interesting for a new man to enter in to the mix."

"I'd think you'd enjoy the attention."

His grin returned. "Oh, I do. I certainly do."

He managed to eat most of the large pizza, and there wasn't an ounce of fat on him that I could see. I'd confined myself to two pieces and hoped all that cheese wouldn't translate itself into an extra inch on my hips by Friday.

It was almost nine o'clock by the time Jeff drove me home. I sat against the passenger door, staring out at the dark streets and thought of all the times some boy had driven me home from a date in high school. I had the same feeling now, that sort of jittery, sick-to-my-stomach sensation, anticipating whether or not he would kiss me, and what I would do if he tried. You'd think, at my age, I'd be over that kind of nervousness, but apparently it had come back to haunt me, like post-adolescent acne.

I had my door open seconds after the truck turned into my drive, but Jeff was almost as quick. "I'll walk you to your door," he said.

He came around the truck and tried to take my arm, but I shied away. "What's wrong?" he asked.

"Nothing." I fumbled in my purse, looking for my keys.

"You've been jumpy all evening. What's your problem? What is it about me that you especially don't like?"

"It's not you in particular," I said, and headed up the walk. "It's just...I haven't had the best of luck with men lately."

"Not all men are jerks like your husband."

I thought of Dr. Patterson and the man who groped me in the elevator. "Just most of the ones I know."

I started to unlock the door, but he covered my hand with his own. "I'm not like them."

I sighed. "You say that, but your mind works like theirs."

"How can you say that? You don't even know me that well."

He was leaning very close, and his eyes were dark with a desire that both frightened and thrilled me. "I know you're probably going to try to kiss me right now," I whispered, any intention I'd ever had of refusing him vanished from my mind.

He took a step back and shook his head. "I don't think so. The mood you're in, you'd probably bite my lips off."

He turned away and I sagged against the door. "Good night, Phoebe," he called when he reached his truck.

When he was gone, I let myself inside. I told myself I'd talked my way out of a tight spot. After all, I really didn't want to start anything with Jeff.

But the part of me that never lied wished I'd let him kiss me.

5

THE NEXT MORNING, I was waiting at Easy Motors when they opened the doors. A teenage receptionist with allergies greeted me with a smile that soon faltered when I told her I'd bought a car there a few days before and now it needed a repair.

"You'll have to talk to Frank," she said, reaching for the phone. "He's in charge of that."

In charge of what? I wondered.

"Mr. A-dams," the receptionist whined into the phone. "We have a customer out here with a prob-lem."

A few moments later, a man in a rumpled brown suit came into the room, hand extended. His grin was too large for his face, wrapping around his cheeks toward his ears. "You're the owner of that little Mustang they towed in last night, aren't you?" he gushed. "Darling car. I can tell by looking it suits you to a tee. Come into my office and we'll fix you right up."

He wrapped his arm around my shoulders and steered me toward a glass-fronted cubicle that reeked of stale cigars and onions. Sweeping aside a stack of dog-eared repair manuals, he pushed me into a folding chair and took his own seat behind a green metal desk. "Now, how can we help you?"

I tried a smile of my own. "It's simple, really. I bought my car here two days ago and last night it broke down. A friend told me it looked like a broken motor mount. So I had it towed here to be fixed."

Friendly Frank nodded and plucked a multipart form from a stack on his desk. "We can do that. We can do that. Fix you right up." He began writing furiously on the form, pausing twice to punch numbers into an ancient adding machine at his side. The machine whirred and clacked and unreeled a stream of yellowed paper. Frank added a final figure and pushed the form toward me. "Sign at the bottom and we'll get right to work."

Numbers danced down the page in cramped script. My gaze fixed on the figure at the bottom. "Four hundred and seventy-two dollars!" I shoved the paper back toward him, gasping for breath. "I'm sorry. I must not have made myself clear. This repair should be covered under the dealer's warranty."

Frank's smile vanished. "Your car is seven years old, and there's no such thing as a warranty on a car that old."

"But I've only had it two days."

He leaned back in his chair, arms crossed over his chest. "I don't make the rules, lady. I just enforce them. Now, do you want the repair or not?"

"Not!" I stood. "I'll take the car somewhere else."

"Fine." He handed me a second form. "That'll be eighty-nine, ninety-seven."

"For what? You haven't done anything."

"Storage fees."

"This is outrageous."

"Don't blame me because you bought an older car. You should have opted for one of our premium models."

"This is not my fault," I protested.

"What do you know about cars, Mrs. Frame?"

I glared at him, but didn't answer.

He rose and patted me on the shoulder. "Do yourself a favor. Next time you go shopping for a car, bring a man along."

I jerked open the door and stormed into the lobby once more. "I want to see the manager," I told the receptionist.

Her eyes widened. "Mr. Adams *is* the manager."

I turned and saw Frank smiling at me. Not the cheery grin with which he'd greeted me, but the look of a sly fox.

I wanted to rip that smile right off his face. I wanted to scream, to throw punches, to do something to make him quit looking at me as if I were a bug and he was about to squash me.

I didn't have the strength to beat him up or the clout to make him afraid of me, so I did the only thing I knew to do. I gave him the haughtiest look I could manage. "This isn't the end of this," I announced, and stomped out the door.

I stalked down the sidewalk, my shoes slapping against the concrete, sending tremors up my legs. My stomach churned and my heart raced. I hated this feeling of helplessness. No matter what Frank said, Easy Motors had cheated me. But there was nothing I could do. They had my car. They had the six thousand dollars I had paid for the car. And unless I gave them more money, I wasn't going to have the money or the car again.

"Aaaargh!" I yelled in frustration. A man on a bicycle stared at me and swerved across the street to avoid me. I didn't care.

I took a deep breath and deliberately slowed my steps. "Don't fall apart, Phoebe," I muttered. "Think this through. There has to be *something* you can do."

I started to feel a little better. I wasn't going to let Frank Adams and Easy Motors get to me. If they were going to fight dirty, then I would fight dirty, too. I didn't have much experience, but I was a fast learner.

MY MOOD HADN'T IMPROVED MUCH by the time I arrived at work, but my co-workers' enthusiastic reaction to my new hair color made me feel a little better. Of course, there's always a spoilsport in every bunch. Joan Lee made a face when she saw me. "I don't think it suits you," she said. "Too flamboyant."

"I can be flamboyant," I protested.

"Transcriptionists are not flamboyant," Joan announced, as if this was a fact obvious to everyone but an idiot.

"Maybe red hair is just a start." I tossed my head in what I hoped was a confident, flamboyant manner. "Maybe I'm thinking of changing careers."

Joan shook her head and walked away. I could see my next job evaluation. *Hair color not suited to job description.*

I filled my coffee mug and headed toward my cubicle. Jeff met me in the hallway. He grinned. "I think there's a flamboyant Phoebe underneath your mild-mannered guise as an ordinary transcriptionist," he said.

The idea pleased me, but I wasn't about to let him know it. I was still a little miffed about the way he'd walked away from me last night. "Didn't anyone ever tell you eavesdropping will get you into trouble?"

He lifted one eyebrow in that sexy way of his. "Maybe I'm a man who likes trouble."

I bit back a smile and hurried past him, to my office. He followed. "Did you get everything settled with your car?"

I tightened my grip on the coffee mug. "Not exactly."

"Not exactly?" He intercepted me in the doorway. "What do you mean, not exactly?"

"The manager at Easy Motors says I don't have a warranty. They want almost five hundred dollars to fix the car, or ninety dollars to release it so I can take it somewhere else."

Jeff frowned. "Want me to go talk to them?"

"No!" Just what I needed, a man getting me out of this fix. "I'll take care of it myself."

He shrugged. "Just thought I'd offer."

I pushed past him and sat at my desk. I dug the phone book out of the drawer and flipped through it. "What are you looking for?" Jeff asked.

"Are you always so nosy?" I punched in a number and waited while it rang.

"*Houston Banner*. Bringing you the news first."

"Hi. I'd like to speak to your consumer affairs reporter."

"I'll transfer you to editorial."

An elevator-music version of "Livin' La Vida Loca" filled my ear. I swiveled my chair around and saw Jeff still watching me. After a moment a man's voice barked, "News desk. Sanborn."

"I'd like to speak to your consumer affairs reporter."

"No such animal."

I blinked. "Pardon me? What happened to Simon Saler, the Consumer's Friend?"

"He quit. Said he wanted to be a sports reporter." I heard a chair squeak and the rustle of papers. "He got tired of people writing in wanting to know where they could buy the last bottle of Coty perfume or complaining they saw a roach run across their table at Casa Lupe."

"My aunt gets her Coty from a specialty store in Dallas. And how would you like it if a roach shared your lunch?"

"Well, why didn't you say something while Simon was still here? Maybe he wouldn't have run off to write about the latest fight on the basketball court."

"But what am I supposed to do about the car dealer who sold me a lemon car?"

"You're on your own, dearie."

Fat lot of help he was. I slammed down the phone. "What are you going to do now?" Jeff asked.

"I'll think of something. Right now, I'd better get started on these charts or Joan will make me clean bedpans or file appeals with insurance companies."

"Go ahead and use your old software to get caught up," he said. "But then I want to start teaching you the new program."

I sat and scowled at the tower of folders beside my monitor, then glanced at the idle computer down the counter from mine. "Joan's going to have to hire someone to help me if she expects me to keep up," I said, and reached for my headphones.

Jeff sat on a stool and rolled it over next to me. "So, are you really contemplating a new career?"

I shrugged. "Maybe." Actually, before that morning, the thought had never occurred to me. Not that I wouldn't enjoy a more glamorous, better-paying job, but transcription was all I was trained for. "I think I'd better handle one life change at a time," I said.

"I didn't realize changing your hair color took that much out of you."

I frowned at him. "I meant my divorce."

"That was six months ago. Old news."

"Which goes to show you've never been divorced."

"I don't intend to be, either."

"What, you're going to remain single all your life?" I slipped the headphones over my head and popped the first tape into the machine.

"No. But when I marry, it's going to be for life."

"That's what I thought, too." I switched on the tape and Dr. Patterson's drawl filled my ears. I didn't want to listen to Jeff's naive pronouncements about the sanctity of marriage. I could have told him no one plans to bail out before "death do us part." Sometimes you just don't see it coming, like a head-on collision. Most people survive, but it doesn't mean you aren't a more careful driver for a while.

He seemed to get the message and left me alone after that. He fiddled with the other computer for a while, then wandered off to some other part of the office. I worked faster once he'd left. There's something disconcerting about listening to a description of an old Mr. Miller's problems with impotence while a sexy stud sits three feet away.

Just before lunch, I finished up a stack of letters to referring physicians and set out to deliver them to the various offices in the building. I could have sent them out with the next batch of interoffice mail, but delivering them in person was one of the few legitimate excuses I had for escaping my cubbyhole.

The last of my letters went to the OB-GYN office on the second floor. Dozens of fruitful women in designer maternity wear kept three physicians and twice as many nurses and techs busy. I could never look at the "wall of fame" beside the reception desk, with its photos of smiling moms and dads with their newborns, without feeling a pang of sadness. I kept telling myself I still had plenty of time to have kids, but there was that pesky matter of needing someone to be the father. I wasn't crazy about diving back into the whole relationship thing any time soon.

"Thanks, Phoebe," the receptionist, Beverly, said when I handed her my letters. "I think I've got some for you, too."

While Beverly went in search of the letters, I turned my back on the family photos and surveyed the waiting room. A trio of women in various stages of pregnancy sat reading copies of *American Baby* and *Modern Maternity*. The nurse came to the door and beckoned one woman and she levered herself out of the chair and waddled toward the exam room. There was something familiar about her long blond hair, her glowing skin....

I clutched the edge of the reception desk, overcome by the urge to scream or puke, I wasn't sure which. The lovely Madonna waddling away from me was none other than Just-a-waitress Tami, the future Mrs. Steven Frame.

"Here are those letters. Thanks for waiting." Beverly

shoved a stack of envelopes toward me. She frowned. "Are you okay? You look a little pale."

"I'm...fine," I lied. In any case, there was no medical cure for what ailed me.

I pretended to look through the letters, trying to collect myself. The print on the envelopes blurred in a haze of rage. A woman waddled up to the desk and handed Beverly some paperwork. "Thanks, Mrs. Alexander," Beverly said. "How are you feeling today?"

"Having a first baby when you're forty is a lot harder than I thought it would be," Mrs. Alexander said. She patted her expanding belly. "But the doctor says I'm doing fine."

I jerked my attention from the letters and stared at her. She was obviously pregnant, but she didn't look like the other glowing young things in the office. Her hair was streaked with gray, and tiny lines radiated out from her eyes. "You're really having a first baby at forty?" I blurted.

She smiled, apparently used to dealing with idiots like me. "Yes. My first husband and I never had children. I thought it was my fault. But when I remarried and my new husband wanted a baby, I thought, why not give it a try?" She laughed. "Turns out there's nothing wrong with me finding another man didn't cure."

She waddled back to her chair and I hurried out of the office. Forty. She was eight years older than me and having a first baby. I still would have gladly strangled Steve if he'd been anywhere in sight, but I felt a little better. I had a lot of good years left. Years to find the right man and start a family.

I boarded the elevator and the only other passenger, a short man with an unfortunately large nose, grinned at me. "Love your hair," he said, letting his gaze drift over me. He reminded me of a basset hound who had just spotted a juicy bone. I expected him to start drooling at any minute.

The elevator stopped at my floor and I rushed out. So much for the "finding the right man" part of the equation. Of course, there was always artificial insemination.

6

THANKS TO THE TIME I'D LOST waiting on Jeff to install my new system and the fact that I was now working alone, I ended up having to stay late at the office several nights. I used to resent those extra hours on the job, but let's face it, if I couldn't improve my social life, I could at least fatten up my bank account with overtime pay.

Besides, there's something mysterious and a little exciting about being at the office after everyone else is gone. It's quiet and you have the whole place to yourself. You can go through people's desks, looking for food and learning their secrets. For instance, I once discovered a pair of crotchless panties in Joan Strictly-Business Lee's desk. I suppose she could have found them in one of the exam rooms, but why would you keep someone else's underwear around?

When no one else was around, you could look through the sample shelves to see what new products were on hand. Not that I'd take any drugs without permission. It was a sure way to get fired and besides, all the really good stuff was kept locked up.

You could play around in the lab, looking at stuff under the microscope and feeling the fake breast to see if you could find the hidden lumps. You could take apart the model of the heart and put it back together again. Granted, none of this would be considered true quality entertainment, but it beat actually working.

Of course, I did eventually have to do some typing. That

was the only creepy thing about working late. Not the work itself so much, but the fact that I was stuck back in my hidey-hole, hooked up to the transcription machine, unable to hear or see anyone approaching. I tried not to think about how vulnerable I was here alone, but, just in case, I always kept a canister of Betadine Spray beside me. It wasn't Mace, but I figured it would at least slow a guy down.

I was well into Patterson's rollicking description of a football scrimmage that resulted in injury to the right wrist of a high school junior when I had the sensation that I was being watched. Goose bumps rose along my arms and the hair on the back of my neck prickled. Patterson's voice still droning in my ear, I grabbed the can of Betadine and swiveled to face the door....

Patterson looked down at the splotch of Betadine quickly spreading across the front of his shirt. "Did I look like I needed disinfecting?" he asked.

"Y—you startled me." I set aside the can and switched off the machine. "What are you doing here?"

"I have a presentation to work on. I'm glad you're here to help me." He began unbuttoning his shirt. I ripped off the headset and reached for the spray can again. I might have known the person who was most likely to give me trouble had a key to the office.

"Put down that can, Phoebe," he said. "I'm only going to change my shirt."

He didn't seem to be in any hurry to do it, though. He stood around for several minutes, apparently hoping I'd be overcome by lust for his naked chest. It wasn't a bad chest, but the fact that it belonged to Patterson made it completely undesirable.

"I like your new hair color," he said. "Red suits you."

"Uh...thanks." I bent over the stack of charts, pretending to search for something.

"Why don't you come into my office and we'll get to work," he said.

As if I was going to fall for that. "I really stayed late to catch up on my transcription," I said. "So I won't be able to help with your project."

"But I really need your help." He put his hand on my shoulder. "I'll see that you're amply rewarded."

I cringed. Did he think sex with him was reward enough, or was he actually willing to pay for time in the sack? I thought about the Viagra I'd flushed and wondered if he was that desperate. Either way, I'd heard enough. "I'm not interested." I shrugged out of his grasp. "Go hit on someone else."

"Phoebe, I'm hurt that you would think me so shallow." He put his hands on my shoulders again and began massaging. "I care about you as a person."

I lurched out of my chair, spray can in hand. "Touch me again and I'll aim for your eyes."

He stepped back, chin jutting out like a kid whose mom just told him he couldn't have another cookie. "I don't appreciate your attitude," he said huffily.

"Well, I don't appreciate yours. Leave me alone or I'll report you."

He glowered at me. "Do that and I'll simply say that you came on to me. Who do you think they'll believe, a redheaded divorcée in a short dress or an esteemed colleague?"

He had me there, though I wasn't about to admit it. "This isn't the 1960s," I said. "Even divorcées in short dresses can have clout, if they talk to the right people." *Like who?* I wondered, but kept that thought to myself. The only way I was going to keep my job and keep Patterson in line was to make him think I knew what I was talking about.

He looked me up and down with an expression of pure contempt, then turned away. "We'll see about that."

I slumped back into my chair, clutching the can of Betadine

to my chest. My heart was pounding so hard I could feel the vibrations through the can. I wanted to run home and take a shower. I wanted to leave this office and never come back.

But why should I do that? I sat up straighter, good old anger blotting out my revulsion. "Why should I let a bully like that push me around?" I muttered.

"Do you always talk to yourself?"

I gasped and whirled around to find Jeff standing in the doorway. "What are you doing here? Don't you have a home to go to?" I snapped.

"I came by to pick up some equipment I left and saw your light." He walked over to the counter and picked up Patterson's abandoned shirt. "Did I come at a bad time?"

"It's not exactly a good time." I slumped in my chair.

He wrinkled his nose. "What's that smell?"

"Betadine. It's a disinfectant."

He looked at the shirt again. "I saw Dr. Patterson in the hallway. He wasn't wearing a shirt."

I didn't say anything. Let him think what he liked.

"Looks like somebody thought the good doctor needed disinfecting."

"Shh." I glanced down the hall. "He'll hear you."

"No, he won't. He left. Didn't look very happy, either." He dropped the shirt into the trash can and leaned back against the counter, facing me. "I think I'm beginning to get the picture."

"You don't know anything." I turned to the computer, but I could still see him, long legs stretched out in front of him, perfectly relaxed. Why shouldn't he be relaxed? He was a man.

"That's a little harsh, don't you think?" He picked up the can of Betadine and studied it. "I'm guessing Patterson got a little fresh and you blasted him. End of story."

As if it were so simple. I glared at him. "If you think that's the end of the story, that shows how much you don't understand."

He crossed his arms over his chest. "Then why don't you help me understand?"

He looked so smug. So sexy. So *young*. How was he ever going to understand how I felt? Anger clawed at my throat, anger at Patterson and Steve and Frank Adams and the anonymous elevator groper and men in general. I stood and poked Jeff in the chest, as if I could poke a hole in that self-assuredness that seemed an inborn thing with men. "No one ever threatened to take your job away if you didn't sleep with them, did they?" I snapped.

He didn't flinch, just kept his irritatingly calm gaze locked to mine. I moved closer, leaning over him, trying to intimidate him. "No one ever turned every conversation they had with you into some kind of sexual word game, did they?" I slid my hand along his thigh and pinched, hard. "No one ever felt you up in an elevator, did they?"

Anger flashed in his eyes and he reached for me, but I darted away. He stood and came toward me and I avoided him. I slipped behind him and circled his throat with my hands, and stood on tiptoe to whisper in his ear. The spicy, exotic scent of his cologne swept over me like a drug. My voice was husky when I spoke. "You never had to be afraid when you went out at night just because you were a man, did you?"

He started to turn, but I put my hands on his shoulders and held him, then slid my hands down the hard column of his back, to that perfectly toned backside. I was breathing hard, anger edged out by fear and manic desire. I was sick of being pushed around by men; now was my time to push back. "No one ever tried to cheat you because you were a man, did they?" I squeezed him, hard, and this time he succeeded in turning to face me.

He reached for me, but I caught his wrists and held them, made strong by the wild emotions that had been building inside me for too long.

I pressed him against the edge of the counter, fitting myself between his straddled legs, pinning his arms alongside him. I could feel his erection against the crux of my thighs and felt distanced from myself, as if the real Phoebe was standing across the room, watching this wild-eyed redhead do these things. "Do you know what it feels like to want to fight back and not be able to?"

I leaned forward and put my lips on his. I don't know what I thought I was doing. Maybe I only meant to excite him and draw away, to frustrate him with the strongest power a woman ever has over most men.

Then I made the mistake of looking into his eyes. What I saw there wasn't fear or loathing, but naked lust. A raw hunger that made me tremble in the deepest part of myself.

Thoughts of revenge and retribution fled, replaced by an overwhelming need. A need to feel, to act, to be alive in a way I hadn't been alive in a long, long time.

We tore at each other's clothes, grappling in our urgency to touch, to taste, to feel each inch of exposed skin. We spoke, not in words, but in sighs and moans, in grunts and soft, throaty murmurs of passion. We traded places and he lifted me to the counter, spreading my legs wide to enter me deeply, fully. I closed my eyes and threw back my head, losing myself in the intensity of the moment. In the distance, I heard a keening cry that rose in pitch and volume. Then I realized I was the one crying, and gave myself up to the sound and the rhythm, riding it like a wave to a collision against emotion and sensation that left me both energized and weakened.

We clung together for a long time afterward, eyes closed, bodies pressed together, until the air conditioner's chill crept over our warmth. I opened my eyes at the first feelings of coldness, and ugly reality descended like a dark cloak.

I struggled away from him and reached for my clothes. I turned away from him, hopping on one foot as I tried to step into my underwear while fighting the urge to run away.

"Phoebe." He reached for me, but I wrenched away.

"I'm sorry," I said, choking on the words. "I didn't mean for that to happen."

"It's all right." He was still naked, standing in the middle of the room as if this was a perfectly normal way to carry on a conversation.

"It's not all right." I found my dress and slipped it over my head, fighting with the zipper.

He put one hand on my shoulder and with the other, drew up the zipper. He gently patted my back. "Don't be upset."

Easy for him to say. Maybe this sort of thing happened to him all the time, but it was definitely a new ball game for me. With shaking hands, I collected my purse. "I have to go."

"I'll take you home." He reached for his trousers.

"No. I'll get a cab."

I ran, taking advantage of the time it would take him to dress. Avoiding the elevator, I headed for the stairs, descending eleven flights and arriving in the lobby breathless and shaking.

I found a taxi and collapsed into the back seat and closed my eyes. Every nerve vibrated with the memory of Jeff's touch. The scents of his cologne, the lingering too-sweet odor of Betadine and the musky aroma of sex clung to me like an invisible garment. My muscles ached from unaccustomed exertion, and a stickiness between my legs reminded me that we hadn't used a condom. Oh, God, what if I ended up pregnant?

I shook my head, refusing to think about that tonight. The

taxi pulled up in front of my house and I handed the driver a ten and didn't wait for my change. All I wanted was to hide in my darkened house, to take a shower and try to convince my-self that I hadn't just made the biggest mistake of my life.

7

IT'S AMAZING WHAT A SHOWER, pajamas and a pint of Ben & Jerry's can do for you. As I scooped out a heavenly spoonful of Bovinity Divinity, I felt my grip on sanity returning.

What you need, I told myself, *is to look at this objectively. Maybe you've made too big a deal of this. You're both adults.* I dug out another spoonful of ice cream.

It's not as if Jeff is some stranger you picked up in a bar. He's made it clear he's interested in you. So what if you took the lead with a man for a change? He didn't seem to mind.

The phone jangled, and I stared at it, heart in my throat. *Oh, God, don't let that be Jeff.* I didn't want to talk to him. I *couldn't* talk to him.

Click. *Hello, this is Phoebe. If this is a telemarketer, leave your number and what time you eat dinner and I'll call you back. If you're calling about a bill, the check is in the mail. If you're a friend, leave a message and I'll call you back.*

"Phoebe. Phoebe, pick up the phone. I know you're home. I want to know what everyone said about your hair."

I let out my breath in a rush and picked up the phone. "Hello, Darla."

"It's about time you answered. What took you so long?"

"I was screening my calls."

"Ohhhh? And why is that?"

"Umm. Didn't feel like talking."

"Come on, Phoebe. Something else is going on. I can hear it in your voice."

I tucked my feet under me and tried to find a comfortable position on the sofa. "Hear what?"

"*Who* don't you want to talk to? A man?"

I sighed. Darla was going to find out the truth sooner or later. I could never keep anything from her. She could have taught the CIA a few things about interrogation. "Jeff," I said.

"Jeff!" Her voice rose in a squeal. "What happened? When? Tell me everything."

I squirmed. "I was working late tonight and Dr. Patterson was there and hit on me again and I'd barely gotten rid of him when Jeff came by and I was really ticked off."

"So you had an argument?"

"Well, sort of."

"And now you're sorry." Darla was full of sympathy. "Don't worry. Apologize tomorrow. Take him to lunch and make nice."

"It's not quite so simple." I twisted a lock of hair around my finger. "We started out arguing and then we sort of...got physical."

I heard the sharp intake of her breath. "Oh, Phoebe, no! Jeff *hit* you?"

"No! Not...not that kind of physical."

The silence was so long I thought maybe we'd lost our connection, then Darla gasped. "Oh! You mean—sex? Right there in your office?"

I nodded. "Uh-huh."

Darla giggled. "So, how was it? Is he a stud or what?"

How was it? My skin tingled from the memory. "It was...wild. I didn't mean for it to happen, it just did. One minute we were arguing and the next we were tearing each other's clothes off."

"Oooh, wild-animal sex. I love it."

"What am I going to do? I didn't mean for it to happen."

"It happened, so go with it. He's a single, good-looking

guy, you had great sex—why not just go with the flow and see where this takes you?"

"He's six years younger than me! We have nothing in common."

"I'd say a strong physical attraction is a good place to start. And what's wrong with a younger man? He's a nice guy, isn't he?"

"He *is* a nice guy. But..." I chewed my lower lip.

"But what?"

"But I don't think I'm ready to get involved with anyone else right now. Every time I turn around these days, some man is trying to take advantage of me. Did I tell you the car dealer is holding my new car hostage?"

"No, and quit trying to change the subject. Just because your ex-husband and your boss are assholes, doesn't mean all men are bad."

"Don't forget the car dealer. And the guy who felt me up in the elevator."

"You got felt up in the elevator? Are you wearing a new perfume or something? Something that drives men wild?"

"I wasn't wearing anything."

"That would do it, too. But isn't it a little chilly?"

How is it someone who drives me absolutely crazy can always make me laugh? "You know what I mean. And you know what I mean about Jeff, too. I don't think jumping his bones at the office is a good way to start off."

"He might not agree with you."

"Exactly. How am I going to face him again and tell him I didn't mean to start anything? That I'm not interested in a relationship or an affair or whatever you want to call it."

"A fling."

"What?"

"You could call it a fling. You know, sowing a few wild oats. After all, you were just a kid when you married Steve."

"Fine. Call it a fling. A one-night fling. Now it's over. But how do I make Jeff understand that?"

"If he works with computers, he must be reasonably intelligent. I'd just tell him."

"Just tell him?"

"Are you having trouble hearing tonight? Yes, just tell him—Jeff, it was great, but I don't want to be involved with anyone right now. Thanks and goodbye. Practice a few times in front of the mirror."

"And you think that'll work?"

"Well, he could always get down on his knees and pledge his undying love for you, but I think that only happens in the movies. Real life is usually more practical."

I took a deep breath. "Okay. I'll do it. Thanks."

She yawned. "No problem. Let me know how it goes. Now I have to get my beauty sleep."

I hung up the phone, collected the empty ice-cream carton and deposited it in the trash. I'd tell Jeff I wasn't interested. It was so logical, so simple. So scary. All I had to do was find the guts to pull it off.

ANY COURAGE I EVER HAD DESERTED ME the next morning, and I took the coward's way out. I called in sick to work. Maybe a day apart would cool things off between me and Jeff. Maybe next time we met, I could face him calmly and take Darla's advice to simply tell him how I felt.

Maybe I'd hit the Lotto jackpot and never have to go back to work again.

Meanwhile, I still had to find a way to get my car back. I poured a cup of coffee, grabbed the phone book and started dialing. Better Business Bureau, American Automobile Association, my insurance agent. I told everyone I could think of my sad story about my car. They all clucked their tongues and shook their heads and basically let me know that I was an idiot who didn't have enough sense to know when I was being cheated. "Maybe you should take the bus from now on," my insurance agent told me. "A car is a big responsibility."

"It's not a dog," I said. "I'm not going to leave it out in the rain to starve."

He made more meaningless sounds of sympathy and told me maybe I should just pay the money to get the car out of hock. "Consider it a lesson learned the hard way."

I slammed down the phone. How many lessons did a person have to learn before she could graduate, or at least move up to the next grade?

I picked up the newspaper and flipped through it, hoping to find notice of a class-action suit against Easy Motors or an ad for a consumer agency that specialized in helping women who'd been swindled.

"Why did Simon Saler have to become a sports writer?" I whined to myself. "*He* would have helped." For the past five years, Simon's homely but friendly face had smiled out at me from the top of his column "Consumer's Confidant." He'd helped people retrieve precious wedding dresses from cleaners who'd skipped town in the middle of the night, gotten a new paint job for a woman who had ended up with a pea-green house and extracted eloquent apologies from multinational corporations that had screwed consumers. He was my hero, and when I needed him, he was gone. Wasn't that just like a man?

Where did the paper get off not hiring a replacement for Simon? Maybe I wasn't having any luck as far as my car was concerned, but I could at least let the paper know how I felt.

I found a pad of paper and a pen and wrote an impassioned plea for the return of the "Consumer's Confidant." I told the whole sorry story of my car, and how no one had been willing to help me. *People think they're justified because they're "following policy" or playing by the rules,* I wrote. *But just because something is legal doesn't mean it's right. I will continue to fight until this wrong is righted.*

I looked at the words on the page. *I ought to cut them out and tape them to the bathroom mirror,* I thought. To remind me that I was on my own now. Nobody else was going to fight my battles for me. Not Steve or Simon Saler or the BBB. I was a one-woman army now.

When I'd finished the letter, I slipped it into an envelope and dropped it in the mail. After a morning of fruitless complaining, writing that letter made me feel as if I'd done something constructive. Maybe it wouldn't do any good, but at least I felt better for having had my say.

By this time, it was after twelve. I debated going out for lunch, but with my luck, I'd run into Joan Lee at Taco Loco and she'd find out the case of stomach flu I'd pleaded wasn't as severe as I thought.

So I settled on a tuna sandwich. I was in the kitchen mixing up the tuna when a sound from the living room made the hair on the back of my neck stand up. I could have sworn I heard a footstep. I froze, spoon poised over the mayonnaise jar, and listened. *Creak...creak.*

What was someone doing in my house in the middle of the day? I looked around for the phone, but the cradle was empty. Then I remembered, I'd taken it into the living room when I was thinking about calling Darla.

I heard the sound of the desk drawer sliding open. Whoever was in there wasn't even trying to be quiet. They probably thought they were alone, that I was at work and they could take their time. Maybe I could use that to my advantage.

I laid aside my spoon and crept across the kitchen to the knife rack and slid the biggest carving knife out of its slot. Then, brandishing the knife like a sword, I tiptoed to the door and eased it open.

A tall, dark figure was hunched over my desk, pawing through the papers. As I watched, he shut the drawer and dumped the pencil cup on the blotter.

"Hold it right there!" I shouted.

Pencils flew everywhere and the cup bounced off the carpet. The bandit yelped and whirled to face me. "Phoebe, what are you doing here?"

I sucked in my breath and stared, goggle-eyed. "Steve?"

8

"WHAT ARE YOU DOING HOME?" Steve sounded annoyed. "You're supposed to be at work." He tilted his head to one side and studied me. "What did you do to your hair?"

I put one hand to my slightly mussed hair, then lowered it, determined not to get sidetracked. "You first. What are you doing breaking into my house?"

"I wasn't breaking in." He dangled his key chain at eye level. "I still have a key." He tucked the keys back into his pocket and frowned. "Put down that knife. You look ridiculous."

I laid the knife aside. It felt ridiculous holding it on him. Even after a year apart, Steve's sudden appearance stirred feelings in me. Not love. Not hate. Just...recognition. I shifted my weight to my right side. Having him here made me nervous. He didn't have a right to be here, and yet, to some part of my brain, he looked at home in the living room we'd once shared. "What's wrong with knocking?"

"I didn't think you were home. Where's your car?" He looked around the room, as if he might find the Probe parked there.

"In the repair shop." Technically true, I suppose. "So you thought I wasn't home and decided to break in."

He stuffed his hands in his pockets and pursed his lips in a look of impatience. "Now, Phoebe, it's not like that." He frowned. "You looked better as a blonde."

"Who asked your opinion?" I smoothed my hair again. "I happen to like it better red."

He shook his head. "You don't have the right personality for a redhead."

"Shows you didn't know me so well after all." Hah! Take that. My smile was downright smug.

Did I mention that Steve is forty-three? He's an accountant at a big oil and gas firm downtown. Wears nice suits, has his thinning hair cut and styled—and I happen to know, colored—at a posh salon in the Galleria. In some ways he's a very handsome man, but I'd learned long ago that he had some very unhandsome attitudes. "Don't try to talk your way out of this one," I said. "You had no right to open that door and you know it." I reached for the phone. "You'd better leave now before I call the police." And after that, I'd call a locksmith. I shuddered. How many times before had he come by when I wasn't home and pawed through my things?

"Now, Phoebe, let's not fight." He crossed the room and took the phone out of my hand as easily as if he'd been taking an empty soda can from a child. "Just because we're divorced doesn't mean we can't be friends."

I suppose I could have put up a fight, screaming and making a scene. Steve hated scenes and he'd always retreat if I threatened one. But he must have come here for a reason and I wanted to find out why. "What are you doing here?" I asked.

He glanced around the living room again, whether avoiding my gaze or searching for something, I couldn't tell. "I came by to get something I left behind when I moved out."

I wrinkled my forehead, puzzled. Steve had carted away a whole moving van full of crap when he moved out. Everything from a drawerful of gym socks to every tool in the garage. Later, when I'd wanted to hang a picture in the living room, I'd had to use the heel of a shoe to hammer in the nail.

"If you're talking about the three-year collection of *Playboy* up in the attic, I threw it away a long time ago."

He winced. "Those could have been worth a lot of money."

"Is that what you were looking for? Old magazines you could sell for a few bucks?" I leaned against the back of the sofa. "Number-crunching business that bad these days?"

He stared at the floor, working his jaw as if trying to get the words out. Finally, he looked at me. "I want the ring."

"What ring?" Every nerve in my body went on red alert. I only had one ring Steve could have been interested in. He wanted his grandmother's diamond solitaire. The ring he had given me when we got engaged. It was a beautiful ring, in a 1920's art deco setting, the one piece of really good jewelry I'd ever owned.

"I want my grandmother's ring."

"My engagement ring." I'd stashed my wedding band in the safe-deposit box the week after the divorce was final and hadn't looked at it since. But I kept the diamond, and still wore it occasionally. I associated that ring with happy times, with young love and the early years, when our marriage had held so much promise.

His lips tightened in a grim line. "That ring is a Frame family heirloom."

An heirloom he hadn't cared one fig about until now, when he was going to get married again. When he was going to have a family. My stomach hurt. "Our divorce decree said all jewelry was mine to keep," I said, my voice tight, strained.

He looked pained. "Phoebe, don't be unreasonable."

"I'm unreasonable? I'm not the one who broke into this house with the intention of stealing my ex-wife's jewelry."

"That was my grandmother's ring."

"It's mine now."

Little beads of sweat sprouted on his forehead. He rocked back and forth on his heels. "I'll pay you for it."

I almost smiled at that. Steve had to be desperate to offer to spend money on me. Just-a-waitress must have heard about the ring and been pressuring him to get it for her. "I don't want your money."

The line of his jaw tightened. "I'll buy you a new ring."

He would buy me a cheap cubic zirconia in a ten-carat setting. I hadn't lived with the man twelve years without learning the way his mind operated. I shook my head. "No. I like *that* ring."

His expression shifted again, to one of desperation. "Phoebe, that ring has great sentimental value to me."

I snorted. "Since when are you sentimental?"

He looked offended. "Becoming a father does that to a man, I guess."

The words were like a match to the anger that smoldered within me. "I thought you didn't want any children," I snapped.

"I've changed my mind."

The truth was there on his face, taking my breath away. He didn't want *my* children. "Get out!" I ordered him.

"No. I'm not leaving until we talk this over like adults."

He still held the phone, but I had an extension in the bedroom. I was on my way to it when the doorbell rang. I went to answer it, grateful for the interruption. After talking with Steve, I probably looked sick enough to fool anyone at the office, and even a delivery person would be a good excuse to get rid of Steve.

The one person I wasn't prepared to find at my door stood grinning at me. "Jeff!" I gasped. "What are you doing here?"

"I brought you some chicken soup." He held up a brown paper bag.

I felt weak in the knees, whether from the reminder of the last time I'd seen him—naked and gorgeous—or the knowledge that now I had to deal with two difficult men at the same time.

"Phoebe, why don't you introduce me to your friend?" Steve had followed me to the door and was smirking at Jeff. I could see that accountant's brain of his assessing Jeff, adding up how old he must be.

"Jeff, this is my ex-husband, Steve. Steve, this is Jeff. He's installing a new transcription service at the office."

Jeff didn't look pleased at that description, but what did he expect? *Steve, this is the man I had wild passionate sex with last night.*

They shook hands, both men doing that guy thing where they try to squeeze the life out of each other's fingers. Judging by the pained look in Steve's eyes, I'd say Jeff won.

Jeff handed me the soup and touched my shoulder. "How are you feeling?"

"I've been better," I said truthfully. And things were getting dicier by the minute. I glanced at Steve. "Steve was just leaving."

Steve smirked. "Anxious for me to go, are you?" He glanced at his watch. "I guess you have to take advantage of these lunch hours, don't you?"

I felt like throwing the hot soup in his face, but that would only prove what he insinuated was true. Instead, I took his arm and urged him over the threshold.

"I intend to get that ring," he said under his breath.

"I won't let you bully me. Not this time."

He left and I shut the door and sagged against it.

"Are you all right?" Jeff asked.

I couldn't think of a good answer. There were days when I thought I might never be all right again.

He looked away, but I didn't miss the look of disgust on his face. "What did you ever see in that guy?"

I pushed away from the door. "Sometimes I ask myself that

question." I carried the soup into the kitchen and he followed. I set the bag on the counter and slumped at the table.

Without asking me, he took the soup carton from the bag and put it in the microwave. Then he hunted through the cabinets and pulled out two bowls. I watched, thinking I ought to protest, but I didn't want to. The truth was, I could use company just now.

And for some reason I felt the need to defend my marriage. To prove that I hadn't been a total idiot to choose Steve in the first place, or to stay with him for all those years. "He was different when we first married," I said.

Jeff didn't look convinced. "What did he want?"

"A ring." I rubbed my finger, where I used to wear the ring all the time. "It belonged to his grandmother, and he gave it to me as an engagement ring. He's getting married again, and I guess he wants it for his new wife."

"And you don't want to give it up."

"Why should I have to give it up?" I slammed my hand onto the table. "Dammit, he took everything else he could get his hands on. He didn't even care about the ring until now."

"Hey, I didn't say you were in the wrong." He sat down beside me, almost, but not quite touching. I was grateful for that. If he'd touched me, I might have broken down.

"I didn't mean to snap at you," I said. "It's just...so frustrating."

"Yeah." His voice had a huskiness to it that made me think he wasn't talking about the ring anymore.

The microwave dinged and he got up and filled the two bowls with soup. He brought them to the table with a waxed-paper sleeve of saltine crackers and two glasses of orange juice. I was reminded of when I was a little girl, and stayed home from school with a cold. This was the lunch my mother had always served me. It was a funny feeling having someone else take care of me, after so many years.

"You'd make a good nurse," I said, only half joking.

"I'm better at fixing computers than people."

We ate in silence, the one thing we hadn't mentioned—the events of last night—hanging like a ghost between us.

Finally, I pushed my empty bowl away. "I'm glad you came over," I said. "This gives us a chance to talk away from the office. About last night—"

"Don't." He put his hand over mine. "If you're going to say anything about how it shouldn't have happened or it was wrong, or anything like that, don't. I wanted it to happen. And I'd have made sure it did, sooner or later."

"Why did you want it to happen?" I looked into his eyes, hoping to find the answer there. What did this gorgeous guy see in me? "You hardly know me. There must be women your own age—"

He smiled. "You act like we're a whole generation apart, instead of a few years." He leaned closer. "How old was your husband?"

I knew what he was getting at, but I knew lying wouldn't do any good. After all, he'd seen Steve. "He's forty-three."

"Eleven years older than you. And that didn't matter to you when you married him."

"How did you know...?"

He grinned. "Michelle told me."

I looked down at the table. "A younger man is different." Even as I said it, I knew it was ridiculous. I slid my chair back and stood, needing to get away from him. "Look, my life is a little screwed up right now. I'm not a person you want to get involved with. What happened last night—"

He held up his hand to stop me, but I pushed on. "It was incredible. Wonderful even. But I can't let it happen again. I have to get my life in order, to figure out what I'm doing here. I don't need another man confusing me."

He stood and came to stand beside me. "At least you admit we were good together. I'll consider that a start."

I stared at him. "Didn't you hear what I just said? I don't want to start anything with you."

"Too late. It's already started." He grinned. "But I'm a patient man." He leaned over and kissed me, the briefest brush of his lips that sent heat coursing through me. "But I'll warn you," he whispered. "I don't play fair. I don't intend to make it easy for you to stay away from me."

9

I HADN'T CONSIDERED what walking into my little workroom the next day was liable to do to me. I strolled in, unsuspecting, cup of coffee in one hand, a doughnut in the other, and the first thing I saw was a stack of papers, the top one wrinkled by what I knew to be my own naked butt. I had perched right there, on the edge of the counter, while Jeff had his way with me.

I flushed at the memory, not with embarrassment, but with a fierce longing to repeat the experience.

Don't be an idiot, I told myself. *Wild, uninhibited sex with a man you hardly know is not a sensible activity for a woman trying to put her life back together.*

Not to mention, if Joan ever found out we'd been doing the dirty on the patient charts, she'd have us both out on the street faster than I could type a resignation letter. I tossed the rumpled chart to one side and dropped into my chair. *Deep breaths,* I reminded myself. *This is just a room. Your workroom. It's not some sexy boudoir.*

Except that all I could smell when I took that deep breath was Jeff's cologne. I grabbed my coffee cup and took a long drink. "God, I'm pathetic," I moaned.

"It can't be that bad."

Coffee sloshed onto my skirt as I squealed. "Jeff! I—I didn't expect to see you."

"But now that I'm here, aren't you glad?" He smiled and held his arms wide.

I looked away, my heart beating double time. I might not enjoy being caught in the middle of all these whirling emotions, but at least I was getting a great aerobic workout.

"You'd better get that out before it leaves a stain." The next thing I knew, he was kneeling in front of me, sponging at my skirt with a handkerchief. If he kept that up, I was going to melt into a puddle right here in this chair.

"Is the air-conditioning on the blink?" I said panting. "It seems awfully warm in here."

He stilled and our eyes met. "Yeah." He licked his lips—gorgeous, moist lips that begged to be kissed. "It is a little warm all of a sudden."

"What are you two doing in here?"

We jumped apart as Joan entered the room. She looked at each of us in turn, lips pursed in disapproval.

"I was just getting ready to start training Phoebe." Jeff stood against the far wall, hands in his back pockets.

I could think of a few things he could train me in...but I pushed that thought aside. "Did you need something, Joan?"

"Doctor wants to see you in his office right away." She turned and left, her heels tap-tapping down the hall.

I shoved up out of my chair. "I'd better go see what he wants."

Patterson was using a pair of surgical scissors to trim his nails when I walked into his office. He gave me a smile that was more of a smirk. "Well, Phoebe, it's nice to see you decided to grace us with your presence today."

I gave myself credit for not making some snide remark just then. But I kept my cool. "Joan said you wanted to see me."

He leaned across the desk and shoved an eight-inch high stack of charts toward me. "I'd like you to transcribe the marked sections of each of these charts for me."

I gaped at the pile of files, which bristled with pink sticky notes. It would take hours...days...to go through all of those.

"I won't be able to get to them right away. I have to train on the new software, and catch up on the work from yesterday."

"Then I guess you'll have to work overtime." He stood and handed me the stack of charts. "I need these for my presentation at the TMA conference."

The charts weighed like a stack of bricks in my arms. "This doesn't have anything to do with my turning down your advances, does it?" I asked, though I already knew the answer.

His expression hardened. "I have no idea what you're talking about. And if I hear any hint of you bringing it up again—to anyone—you will be out of a job."

My stomach clenched. I had no doubt Patterson would carry out that threat without blinking an eye. "Yes, sir," I said through clenched teeth.

I walked as fast as I could back to my office and tossed the files onto my desk, sending them skidding across the counter to collide with the monitor where Jeff now sat.

He looked up, one eyebrow raised. "Something wrong?"

"Patterson's given me all this extra work to do. I think he's trying to get back at me for turning him down the other night."

"Why don't you just report him for sexual harassment? File a complaint with the Medical Society or something?"

I slapped my hand against my forehead. "Gee, why didn't I think of that?" I gave him a withering look. "I'm not totally stupid, you know."

He swiveled to face me. "Then why don't you do it?"

"Oh, sure." I picked up the phone and spoke into the receiver in my best Miss Priss voice. "Hello, Harris County Medical Society? I'd like to report that one of your members seems to think boinking the boss is part of my job description. Yes, the doctor has a fine reputation as a physician. Me? I'm a transcriptionist. Yes, I'm divorced. My skirt? I'm not sure the length of my skirt has anything to do with this. Did I ever encourage the doctor's advances? Absolutely not! Oh, but he says I did? He said what? That in the aftermath of my divorce, I turned to him for advice and comfort? That's ridiculous! Well, no, I don't think anyone actually *saw* the doctor make advances toward me. Yes, it is my word against his. Yes, I suppose you're right."

I hung up the phone and looked at Jeff. "The Medical Society is one of the biggest old-boy networks around. Believe me, they're going to look after their own, and a complaint by one lowly transcriptionist isn't going to mean anything to them."

He frowned. "I think you're exaggerating. After all, there are women in the Medical Society, too. Surely they'd take your side."

I shook my head. "They're doctors first, then women. They had to be to get as far as they have. Not only that, a lot of them are married to doctors and they live in fear of women like me seducing their husbands." I pulled out my keyboard drawer and slid a pile of charts toward me. "If I complained, all I'd end up with is a reputation as a troublemaker and a spot in the unemployment line."

"So what are you going to do?"

I shrugged. Hadn't I just told him there was nothing I could do? It wasn't as if I liked being helpless. But in this case, I knew I was. "I'm going to avoid being alone with the good doctor and watch my back."

He slid his chair over next to mine. "I'll be keeping an eye on Patterson, too. If he lays a hand on you, I'll bust his chops."

Oh, boy. I took a deep breath. I should have seen this coming. Men are *so* predictable sometimes. I mean, they sleep with you once and suddenly they're like cavemen, beating their chests and booming "You my woman now." I looked down my nose at Jeff, doing my best impression of every stern schoolteacher I'd ever had. "There's something we need to get straight right now," I said. "What happened the other night, in here, doesn't give you any kind of claim on me. And it doesn't give me any claim on you. Understand?"

He nodded, but the knowing look in his eyes said he didn't really believe it. *Oh, God, a romantic! That was worse than a caveman. Now he probably thought because lust had got the better of our common sense, we were meant for each other.*

"Quit looking at me that way!" I snapped.

"What way?" A smile tugged at the corners of his mouth and he scooted his chair even closer.

"Like you're thinking nasty thoughts about me."

The smile came out full force and he waggled his eyebrows. "Maybe I am."

I laughed. How could I keep from it when he looked so silly—part sexy stud, part endearing boy? "All right, Prince Charming," I said when my giggles subsided. "Why don't we get to work?"

For the rest of the morning, we worked side by side as he showed me the ins and outs of the new transcription software. I'd expected working with him again would be awkward, but I actually enjoyed myself. Jeff was a good teacher, much more patient than I would have been.

Yes, I was very much aware of him—of his thigh brushing against mine when he leaned forward to show me how to adjust the volume; of his breath, warm on my neck when he prompted me to hit the command keys; and of his cologne, filling my senses with memories of those wild, passionate moments in his arms. But that heightened awareness was like the thrill of a roller-coaster ride without the danger. Desire buzzed through me like an electric current, making me feel that much sharper, more alive, ready for anything.

I had just aced my fourth tutorial when he reached out and

snagged my hand in his. "Is this the ring?" He stroked his thumb across the diamond.

"That's the one." I eased out of his grasp and held my hand up to the light. "Isn't it beautiful?"

"It's beautiful on you."

I quickly looked away from his out-and-out admiration, which had gotten me into trouble in the first place. For whatever reason, this young guy found me attractive, but that was no reason to lose my head, or to think that anything positive could come from this.

"It's time for lunch," I shoved back my chair and stood.

"Let's go somewhere together." He stood also. "I hear the Warwick has a great café downstairs."

And great bedrooms for rent upstairs, I thought. I shook my head. "I have some errands to run." I slipped my purse over my shoulder and got the hell out of there, before the bedroom-eyed boy made me change my mind.

Only one elevator was working today. I wondered who'd got caught in the other one this time. Word was one of the neurologists had been trapped last week and missed his tee time. He was threatening to sue the building owners.

The working elevator's doors parted and Darla hurried out and almost bowled me over. "Ready for lunch?"

10

DAMN. I'D FORGOTTEN TODAY was Thursday, my regular date with Darla. "I don't have time for lunch," I told her. "I have to get over to the car lot."

I started toward the open elevator, but she put a hand on my shoulder, holding me back. We watched the doors slide shut and the elevator descend without us. "You have to eat."

"I really have to get over to the car dealer." I punched the down button again.

"She wouldn't go to lunch with me, either."

Jeff came up behind us and put one hand on my shoulder. Darla's smile widened and a slightly dazed look came into her eyes. "Who are you?"

"Darla, this is Jeff. Jeff, this is my best friend, Darla." I watched, getting a good look at Jeff from Darla's point of view, as a stranger, without prejudices. Well, except that she knew he and I had had sex, and that it had been a fantastic experience, but not one I wanted to repeat.

The truth was, Jeff was a damn good-looking man. Not movie-star handsome, but real-man handsome, with a strong jaw, thick hair, just the right amount of muscle and a way of looking at a woman that made her feel like Eve and Aphrodite and Princess Diana, all rolled into one.

"Well, *I'd* certainly go to lunch with you," Darla cooed. The elevator arrived again and the doors split open. "But right now, Phoebe and I have some things to talk about." She grabbed my hand and pulled me onto the open elevator.

She waited until we'd descended three floors before she spoke. "I can see why you jumped his bones. What a hottie!" She fanned herself.

"Jeez, Darla. You make it sound like *I* seduced *him*."

"From the way you described it to me on the phone, it was a mutual seduction."

I folded my arms under my breasts. "It was nothing of the sort. It just...happened."

"Uh-huh. You know, you really need to learn to be more comfortable with your sexuality. There was a doctor on *Oprah* the other day who was talking about just this thing...."

By the time we reached the lobby, I had a list of three books and two movies I should read or view to rid myself of my latent guilt about my sexuality.

We bought hot dogs from a street cart and walked over to the fountain in front of the Warwick Hotel to eat them. It was one of those rare fall days when the weather in Houston is perfect. The muggy heat of summer has faded and the damp chill of winter hasn't yet set in. Office workers had turned out in droves to enjoy the sunshine and cool breezes. A busker was playing energetic blues by the fountain, his open guitar case littered with change from an appreciative audience.

"Your hair looks great," Darla said as we waited in line for our dogs.

"Thanks." I couldn't help but smile. "I never got this much attention when I was a blonde."

"Maybe it's not the hair. Maybe it's the new Phoebe. The improved, kick-ass version."

I laughed. "Right. I think it's the hair. I haven't done much ass kicking lately."

"I don't know about that. The old Phoebe would never have had her way with a gorgeous hunk like Jeff."

I blushed. "Don't remind me." I still couldn't believe I'd gone after him the way I had. Or that it had felt so good.

We took a seat beside the water. "So what's Jeff like?" Darla asked. "Is he a nice guy?"

I shrugged. "He's nice." I took a bite of hot dog and chewed thoughtfully. "Too charming for his own good," I added after I'd swallowed.

"I like him. You shouldn't worry about the age difference or what people think." She popped a bite of hot dog into her mouth. "Or what Steve thinks. Not that he even has to know about it. It's none of his business who you go out with."

I winced. "He already knows. I mean, not that Jeff and I are dating—which we aren't. But I think he suspects something is going on. Which it isn't."

"Steve knows about Jeff?" Her eyes widened. "How did he find out?"

"Jeff came to the house when Steve was there and they didn't exactly hit it off."

"Oooh, two stallions fighting over the mare. I'll bet *that* was interesting."

"I am not a mare. And I'd hardly call Steve a stallion." Jeff, on the other hand...

Darla waved aside my protest. "I was speaking figuratively. I just heard a guy on the radio. He's written a new book that explains all human relationships in terms of the behavior of farm animals." She leaned toward me. "Did you know that pigs have the longest orgasms of all domestic animals?"

"And what am I supposed to do with that little tidbit of information?" I shook my head in exasperation. "If Steve and Jeff behaved like animals, it was more like two grumpy bears."

"What was Steve doing at your house anyway? Did you invite him over?"

"God, no! He broke in."

"He broke in?" Darla's shriek sent three pigeons fluttering

into the air. A woman across from us looked up from her book and frowned. Darla made a face at her and turned back to me. "Steve actually broke into your house? Why?"

"He wanted his grandmother's ring." I held out my hand, showing her the jewel in question. "It was my engagement ring and the divorce settlement gave it to me, but now that he and Just-a-waitress are getting married, he wants it back."

"Tell the cheapskate to go buy a new ring." Darla wadded her hot-dog wrapper into a ball. "And Jeff came by in the middle of this? Just paying a social call?"

"I called in sick to work and he stopped by to check on me."

"That's so sweet. I told you I liked him." She patted my arm. "See, Tony isn't the only nice guy left in the world."

I frowned at the remains of my hot dog. My feelings about Jeff were too mixed-up for me to talk about right now. I didn't even want to think about them. Why did relationships have to be so complicated? "Darla, do me a favor," I said. "Just shut up. Okay?"

She grinned. "You do have it bad, don't you?"

I glared at her, but she kept right on grinning, as if she knew something about me even I didn't know yet.

THAT AFTERNOON, I HEADED OVER to Easy Motors for another try at freeing my car. I armed myself with a list of places I'd filed complaints, and a T-shirt I'd had made up that read I Bought a Lemon at Easy Motors. I'd wanted it to read Easy Motors Cheats Customers but the clerk at the T-shirt store had persuaded me that the car dealer could sue me for that, whereas stating I bought a lemon from them was closer to fact. "Are you a law student?" I asked as I paid for my finished shirt.

He grinned. "Nah. I watch a lot of Court TV."

Hector was on the lot with a customer when I walked up,

and he about dropped his teeth when he saw my shirt. The black shirt with fluorescent green lettering was hard to miss. He left his potential buyer and hustled over to me. "You can't wear that here," he growled.

I tried not to look as nervous as I felt. "It's a free country. And I'm merely stating the truth." I looked around the lot. "Where is my car, by the way?"

He looked evasive. "You'll have to ask Frank about that."

"Good, I'll do that." I marched to the office, past the gaping secretary, and into Frank's office. He was just about to bite into a meatball sub when I burst through the door, and my sudden entrance sent a meatball spurting out the side to roll across his desk.

"You!" He stood, still clutching the sandwich in one hand. "What are you doing here? And get that shirt off!"

"Do you think my being topless would distract the customers from the fact that you're cheating them?"

His face was the color of the sauce oozing out the sides of the sub. "It's bad enough you write to the papers, now you come around here harassing us, too. I'll call the police." He reached for the phone.

"The papers?" I blinked. "What are you talking about?"

"They printed your letter in today's edition." He punched in three numbers and barked into the phone. "I want a cop over here right away. I've got a customer who's making trouble."

The words sent a jolt of fear through my middle, but I told myself the police wouldn't take such a complaint seriously. Besides, I wanted to find out more about my letter in the paper.

While Frank mumbled into the phone, I leaned over and looked into his trash can. Sure enough, peeking out from beneath a fast-food wrapper was this morning's edition of the *Houston Banner*. I fished it out and stared down at the editorial page, with my letter displayed prominently in the middle. *Woman distressed over poor treatment at car dealership* read the headline.

My smile got bigger the more I read. There were my words, in print for everyone to see. Or at least everyone who read the paper. And there was my name at the bottom. Phoebe Frame. It had never looked so good. Not even on a check.

The door opened behind me and one of Houston's finest strolled in. He was the poster-boy image of a cop, the kind you see on TV shows: young, tall, muscular, of an indeterminate but decidedly ethnic background. He looked slightly annoyed at having been called out on this piddly call. "Mr. Adams? You having some sort of problem here?" He glanced at me and I gave him what I hoped was a friendly smile.

"No problem, officer," I said. "I just came to talk to Mr. Adams about my car."

The officer glanced at my shirt and grinned. "I read about you in the paper." He turned to Frank. "Why don't you just give this lady her car back?"

Frank squared his shoulders and tried to look dignified, but since he was still holding the limp meatball sandwich in one hand, the effort was wasted. "If she wants her car back, she can pay me three hundred and fifty-nine dollars and eighty-eight cents in storage fees."

"Three fifty-nine?" I squeaked. "You told me eighty-nine, ninety-seven before."

"That's eighty-nine, ninety-seven a *day*." He shook his head. "I ain't running no parking garage here."

"It seems to me you two ought to be able to come to some kind of compromise," the cop said.

"He's holding my car hostage," I said.

"I won't be bullied by a customer." Frank jabbed his finger toward me. "Now I want you to escort her off my property this minute."

"You don't have to do that." I laid the paper back down on Frank's desk. "I was just leaving." I laid my list of complaint organizations alongside the paper. "Here's a list of places with whom I've filed complaints about Easy Motors. I imagine you'll be hearing from them soon." I waggled my fingers at the two men and sauntered out of the office. If I swayed my hips just a little more than necessary, it was only because I was feeling pretty satisfied with myself. I didn't have my car back yet, but I hadn't let myself be bullied into accepting something that was blatantly wrong, either.

Outside, I raised my fist in the air triumphantly. "I have not yet begun to fight," I said.

A taxi mistook my victorious gesture and screeched to a halt in front of me. What the heck? I climbed in back and told the driver to take me to the closest newsstand. I needed about twenty copies of today's issue of the *Houston Banner*.

I TOOK TEN COPIES OF MY ARTICLE to work on Monday and, for about five minutes, everyone was impressed. Then one of the drug pushers came in with fresh Krispy Kreme doughnuts and I was old news. I took a copy of the paper and a fresh doughnut back to my work space and ate while admiring my words all over again.

Jeff wasn't around today. He had another client to take care of. And here I thought I was the only one! Though I didn't like to admit it, I missed him. Aside from the fact that I wouldn't consider dating him, I'd begun to think of him as a friend. At least I could talk to him and he listened and even seemed to respect my opinion about things. But maybe that was only because he wanted back in my pants. You never can tell with men.

About ten o'clock, I was the office celebrity all over again when a florist's delivery came for me. The arrangement of sweetheart roses and carnations was sweet and showy at the same time, and brought out a satisfying chorus of envious oohs and ahs and jealous looks from my coworkers.

"Who's it from?" Michelle asked as I unpinned the card from the pink satin ribbon around the vase.

My heart beat wildly as I slit open the envelope. Would it be too much to hope they were from Jeff? But then, everyone would give me a hard time about it and Joan might feel compelled to lecture me on the office policy on relationships with contractors—which no one knew about but her.

I took a deep breath and read the card. "From a secret admirer." A thrill ran through me and I squinted at the handwriting. Did Jeff make his *S's* like that?

"Ooh, how exciting!" Barbara peered over my shoulder. "Who do you think it is?"

I shook my head. If Jeff wanted to send me flowers, wouldn't he say so? He hadn't been shy about declaring his feelings before now.

"Maybe a patient has a crush on you," Michelle said.

"Or a friend?" Joan snatched the card from my hand and turned it over. "It's from Casa Verde florist. Why don't you call and ask them who sent them?"

"I already thought of that." I grabbed the card and stuffed it back in the envelope. Actually, I hadn't thought of it before she said anything, but I'm sure I would have.

I picked up the flowers and carried them back to my office. Then I dialed the number for the florist. "Hi, my name is Phoebe Frame and someone from your shop just delivered some flowers to me at the Central Care Network Clinic—Dr. Patterson's office.... Oh, yes, they're beautiful. I love them. But the card doesn't say who they're from and I wondered... Yes, I'll hold."

I hummed along with the Indigo Girls and admired the waxy sheen of a pink rose in the arrangement. What is it about getting flowers that makes a woman feel so special?

Would a man feel the same way if I sent him a bouquet? I shook my head. No, men appreciate something they can eat or wear.

"Hello?" The florist clerk came back on the line. "Those flowers were ordered by a man named Eddie."

I frowned. "Eddie who?"

"Doesn't say. Just Eddie. I wasn't here when he came in."

"It doesn't ring a bell, but thank you." I hung up the phone and looked again at the card that had come with the flowers. Who the heck was Eddie and why was he sending me flowers? I buried my nose in the bouquet and sniffed appreciatively. What the heck? I might as well enjoy them while I could. Whoever he was, Eddie was obviously a man with excellent tastes.

I set the flowers up on the filing cabinet and stepped back to admire them. The only thing better would be if Jeff were here to see these. *I wonder if he'd be jealous?*

11

I DECIDED AS LONG AS I had the ring out, I ought to get it cleaned and appraised. If Steve made any more offers, I could come back at him with the true value—a price I was pretty certain he was too cheap to pay.

The only jewelry store I knew that did appraisals was in the Galleria. This is the fanciest mall in Houston, home to Neiman Marcus, Nordstrom, Saks and an indoor ice rink. When you get tired of looking at all the high-dollar items for sale, you can sit at tables overlooking the rink and watch all the would-be Tara Lipinskis practicing their spins and leaps.

The old jeweler's eyes lit up when I showed him the ring. "Oh, yes, a very fine piece." He put his fingers on either side of the band. "May I?"

I let him slip it off. He fished a loupe from his pocket and fit it to his eye. "Art deco," he said. "Possibly even Tiffany. The stone has a very fine color and a nice cut." He raised his eyes and handed the ring back to me. "If you'd like to sell it, I could offer you five thousand for it."

I blinked. That much, huh? Steve would never shell out that much cash for this when he could buy Just-a-waitress a new one for half the price. "No thank you," I said. "It has a lot of sentimental value for me. But I would like to have it cleaned."

While he took the ring into the back to clean it, I wandered through the shop, admiring all the necklaces, bracelets and earrings I'd never be able to afford. Still, it was nice to dream....

A young couple walked in, holding hands. She had the blond, blue-eyed good looks and fresh-faced complexion of a high school cheerleader and the business suit he wore didn't fit him as well as his old football uniform probably had. I could read their whole story on their faces: high school sweethearts, he was out of college now and working in his first real job. They'd just gotten engaged and had come in to pick out a ring.

Sure enough, they stopped in front of the display of wedding sets. A grandmotherly clerk greeted them with a smile, then offered congratulations.

I drifted away, not wanting to intrude on this private moment. But I couldn't help glancing back toward them. The clerk pulled out a tray and the girl oohed and aahed over the selection. After a moment, she pointed to one and her young man removed it from the slot in the case and slipped it onto her finger.

The light in her eyes illuminated them both. He looked at her with a besotted expression and then they kissed, a sweet, tender touching of their lips I had to look away from.

I blinked back tears, cursing my sudden turn toward sentimentality. Steve and I had probably never looked that sappily at each other. Maybe that was the problem.

"Mrs. Frame, I have your ring now." I accepted the ring from the clerk. The stone shone with blinding brilliance. It looked like a ring worth five thousand dollars and I was tempted to keep my hand covered as I walked down the street, lest anyone try to steal it.

I glanced down the counter at the young couple once more. She was holding out her hand, admiring the simple solitaire on her ring finger. Her ring probably wasn't worth a third of mine, but I knew she'd never trade places with me for a whole roomful of diamonds.

AFTER I LEFT THE JEWELRY STORE, I decided to have a look around the mall. I hadn't been here in a long time, though once it had been my favorite hangout. As I said before, it had all the poshest stores, and that magical wonderland atmosphere that all the best malls have. As if everything you needed to make dreams come true could be found somewhere amongst the rows and rows of brightly lit stores.

When I was a little girl, my family would make a special trip to the Galleria each Christmas, to visit Santa Claus and to look at all the decorations: towering nutcracker soldiers and giant golden angels, a Christmas tree as tall as a building, covered with candy garlands and lavish ornaments and a little train that gave rides around Santa's village.

Even in the middle of summer, the Galleria still had some of that Christmas magic for me. When I was a teenager, Darla and I came here almost every Saturday. We'd check out the latest sales at The Limited and Gap, then head to the ice-skating rink. Even when it was a broiling one hundred degrees outside, the ice rink was cool, in every sense of the word.

My girlfriends and I would wear our shortest skirts to skate, and when a cute guy was around, we'd twirl and twirl, until we were dizzy. The boys would hang out along the side of the rink and watch, hoping to catch a glimpse of the girls' underwear.

I stopped and watched a teenage girl skate a lazy figure eight. She looked so young and graceful, with her long brown hair flying out behind her. The kind of girl the guys would stop and watch.

Funny, I hadn't thought about skating in years. I wondered if I could even stand up on the ice anymore. Steve hadn't liked to skate, so we'd never come here after we started dating.

I watched the girl turn and head back up the ice toward me. Why had I let Steve keep me from something I'd enjoyed so much? I tightened my grip on the railing around the rink. I wasn't going to do that anymore. I wasn't going to let anyone else decide what I would do or not do. I'd do the things I wanted and if they didn't like it, they could lump it.

MY MOTHER USED TO SAY "trouble comes in threes" but in my case it was more like multiples of three. An ordinary day for me meant at least one minor crisis, and lately I'd had more than my share of major ordeals. If there's any kind of balance in the universe, somewhere my alter ego is sailing through life completely untouched by chaos.

This thought didn't give me much comfort, however, the morning I reached up to adjust my shower and the showerhead broke off in my hand. As hot water cascaded over me, I screamed and groped blindly for the faucet. "Stop! Stop! Stop! Aaaargh!"

By the time I had the water shut off, my bathroom was flooded. I pushed my wet hair out of my eyes and stared up at the jagged end of the pipe that protruded a scant quarter inch from the wall. I looked at the equally jagged end of the showerhead in my hand. "Something tells me Super Glue isn't going to be enough to fix this."

I finished rinsing off under the tap, then dried off and went in search of the phone book. Houston has plenty of plumbers. I flipped to the last page of the listings and called Zaragosa Plumbing. My theory is that AAA Plumbing and Acme Plumbing get all the business from the people who are too lazy to look any further. I thought if I picked someone whose name began with a Z, I might have a chance of getting him to come to my house before next Christmas.

I explained my problem to the woman who answered the phone. "He can take a look at it this afternoon," she said.

"What time this afternoon?" I asked.

"He don't have a schedule like a bus. This afternoon is as close as I can get."

"Oh. It's just that I have to work." If I took another day off, Joan was liable to have a full-blown conniption.

"And you think maybe Mr. Zaragosa spends his afternoons down at the bowling alley? You ain't the only woman in Houston with plumbing problems, lady. The city's eat up with bad pipes."

I thought about telling the woman that Mr. Zaragosa wasn't the only plumber in Houston, either, but I had a feeling I wasn't going to have much better luck with someone further up in the alphabet. "All right. Tell him to come by this afternoon." I gave her the address, then went to get dressed for work.

My luck wasn't all bad that day. City buses were on time for a change and I showed up at the office with a full minute to spare. I had just about worked up the courage to tell Joan I needed the afternoon off, when Michelle told me the dragon lady had a dentist appointment after lunch. Back in my cubbyhole, I did a victory dance. Saved by tooth decay.

At twelve twenty-two I ran up the walk and fitted the key into my front-door lock. Surely the plumber had stopped for lunch and I'd have time to grab a bite before his arrival.

I could have prepared and eaten a five-course meal before the Zaragosa Plumbing truck rattled into my driveway at three forty-five. A short, thick man climbed out of the cab. His black T-shirt barely fit over the muscles of his arms, and even the denim overalls he wore strained against his broad chest. Wrenches, pieces of pipe and a large hammer poked up out of the top of the canvas tool bag he carried. "Mrs. Frame?" he asked.

"Yes. Thank you for coming."

He stuck out a meaty hand. "Vince Zaragosa. I understand you got a problem with your shower."

"Yes. It's right back here."

I showed him the busted showerhead. He turned it over in his hand and shook his head. "I'm betting these pipes are pretty old."

"The house was built in seventy-eight," I said.

He nodded. "What did I tell you?"

I watched from the doorway as he planted both feet in my bathtub and stared up at the pipe protruding from the wall.

"Can you fix it?" I asked anxiously.

He looked back over his shoulder at me. "Lady, I can fix anything but a broken heart."

I figured, on that note, I'd better leave him to his work. I retreated to the kitchen and cracked open a Diet Coke. I wondered how much this was going to cost me. I'd heard plumbing was expensive.

I was still musing on this when Vince Zaragosa strolled into the kitchen. He laid a faucet handle in front of me. "This was gonna go any minute," he said. "You'd better let me replace both handles and the spigot, too."

I stared at the round, faceted handle. "Um, how much is this going to cost?"

"Less now than if you wait until you've got water spewing all over the place and I have to come out here at night or on a Saturday on an emergency call."

"How much?"

He wiped his hands on a rag and stuffed the rag into his back pocket. "The whole thing, like new, two hundred and eighty-seven dollars."

I swallowed. "Oh, wow."

"You think that's too much? It's one of the best rates in

town. Those guys over at Acme would charge you three twenty-five and not even blink an eye."

I stood up, so I could look him in the eye. Since we were almost the same height, this was easy. "Mr. Zaragosa, are you being straight with me?"

"Straight as a preacher," he said solemnly.

I swallowed. "Because I have to tell you, I've heard of cases where repairmen take advantage of women because we don't have any good way of checking out what you're telling us."

"You think I'm taking advantage of you because you're a woman?"

"I'm not saying that's what you're doing. I'm saying it's been known to happen."

He nodded, and started muttering in Spanish. *Oh, God, I've done it now,* I thought. *I've offended him.* He'll tell every plumber in Houston about this, and I'll be washing my hair under the faucet for the rest of my life.

"Let me show you something." He pulled his wallet from his back pocket and flipped it open. I figured he was going to take out his license and make some speech about his integrity. Instead, he unfolded a string of photos that cascaded almost to the floor. "This is Seraphina, my oldest daughter." He pointed to a smiling girl in a graduation cap and gown.

"This is Lucinda. That's her wedding picture. And that's Estelle and the twins Maria and Sophia. The last picture there is the baby, Pilar."

I admired the photos. "They're all very pretty. But, uh, what does this have to do with my plumbing?"

He refolded the pictures and replaced the wallet in his pocket. "I have six daughters, Mrs. Frame. And the woman you talked to on the phone? That's my wife, and you probably figured out, she don't take nothing off nobody. You think a man who has to answer to seven women is going to try to get away with cheating one?"

I smiled, and he smiled back. "I guess not," I said. "Do you take Visa?"

An hour later, I was the proud owner of all-new shower fittings. "They give you any problems, you call me back," Mr. Zaragosa said as he packed up his tools.

"Thanks." I signed the charge slip and handed him his copy. "And thanks for not getting upset when I questioned the charges."

He waved away my apology. "I know you were just looking out for yourself." He handed me his card. "You need anything else, you let me know."

I looked down at the card and laughed. There, in black letters beneath his name, was a slogan. I Can Fix Anything But a Broken Heart. "Goodbye, Mrs. Frame," he said as he stepped out the door. "You take care, and remember, not every man is out to take advantage of you. There are still some of us good guys left."

JEFF WAS SUPPOSED TO COME BACK to the office the next week to continue training me, but he sent a message that he had to go out of town. I was sick with disappointment. I didn't want to care about him, but obviously the guy had really gotten under my skin.

But then, most of my feelings were contradictory these days. I found out for sure that I wasn't pregnant from my wild night of whoopee with Jeff. I should have been overjoyed, but instead I burst into tears as I hunted under the counter for the box of tampons. Even single motherhood sounded better than no motherhood at all, and at the rate I was going, I might never find a guy decent enough to marry, not to mention love.

I blamed Steve. Why not? He had behaved like a jerk and deserved all the blame I could heap on him. After all, he'd been the one who didn't want a family, who had swept me off my feet when I was young and vulnerable, then abandoned me when some of that youth and vulnerability faded.

A week after my visit to the mall, I received a certified letter from a lawyer, along with a proposed "resettlement" which granted Steve the right to his grandmother's ring and me four thousand dollars.

I read the letter twice to make sure I understood it. Steve must want the ring pretty badly to fork over that kind of cash. But I didn't care about the money. That ring was mine and he had no right to take it away.

I wadded the letter into a ball and launched it toward the kitchen trash. Two points!

Then I went and fished it out and smoothed out the wrinkles the best I could. Not that I intended to take him up on the offer, but you never know when a letter like that might come in handy.

I looked around my desolate living room. Friday night and here I was all alone. There was only one thing to do: time for a pity party.

Like any good shindig, the success of a pity party hinges on food and entertainment. Fortunately, I had all the ingredients close at hand: ice cream (the good stuff, none of that diet stuff will do), hot fudge, popcorn with extra butter and wine of your choice. I prefer a nice Pinot Grigio, but if you're going for the pizza and cheese-curl party food, a nice Lambrusco goes well.

For entertainment, I raided my stash of videos. The weepier, the better. *An Affair to Remember, Titanic, Casablanca.*

I put on my flannel jammies, popped the corn, dished up the ice cream, poured the wine, grabbed a box of tissues and punched the play button. Who needs real men when you've got Cary Grant, Leonardo DiCaprio and Humphrey Bogart right in your living room?

I'd just reached the scene where Humphrey Bogart tells Ingrid Bergman they'll always have Paris when the phone rang. I started to let the machine get it, but hoping it was Darla—or maybe Jeff, not that I really cared, of course—I snatched up the receiver on the third ring. "Hello?"

"Is this Phoebe Frame?" asked a masculine voice on the other end of the line.

I frowned. "Who wants to know and what are you selling?" Didn't these phone solicitors ever take a night off?

"Mike Dawson from the *Houston Banner*. I wanted to see how it's going with your fight against Easy Motors. Do you have your car back yet?"

I set aside my half-eaten dish of ice cream and hit the pause button on the video. "No. They're still holding it hostage."

"Have you talked to them since we published your letter?"

"I went by there the day the letter came out. The manager had a copy of the paper in his trash can. He wasn't too happy to see me, I tell you."

"What did he say?"

"He called the police and tried to have them haul me away." I smiled at the memory of Frank's red face. "The officer just asked him why he didn't release my car."

Mike Dawson laughed. "What would you think of going over there again tomorrow, with me and a photographer? I'd like to do a follow-up story for the paper. Our readers really love this kind of thing."

"What kind of thing?" A woman making a fool of herself?

"You know, David and Goliath. The underdog fighting the big company."

I didn't think Easy Motors was exactly a "big company" but I got his drift. "Sure, I'll go back over there," I said. "I'm not giving up until I get my car back."

"That's the spirit. I'll meet you there tomorrow morning at eleven."

I hung up the phone and stared at the bowl of melting ice

cream. I had just agreed to have my picture in the paper. I was going to let the whole city, including the many people who never read the letters in the editorial section, know that I'd been made a fool of by both my ex-husband and a sleazy used-car dealer. Oh, God, what was I thinking?

I shut off the video and slumped down on the sofa. I could not go tomorrow. The reporter could do the story without me. He could talk to Frank, take pictures of the dealership...

And I'd be sitting here without a car.

Or I could go. I could wear my Lemon T-shirt and tell my side of the story to anybody who'd listen and maybe, just maybe, I'd do some good. Maybe I'd even get my car back. At the very least, I'd show Easy Motors that I wasn't a pushover.

I drained my wineglass and carried the melted ice cream into the kitchen. Forget the movies. I had to get ready for tomorrow. I was David going into battle and I needed to marshal my forces and plan my attack.

At the very least, I needed to wash my hair and do my nails for my media debut. A woman has to have her priorities straight, after all.

12

THE NEXT MORNING, I met Mike Dawson and the photographer, Sheila Mills, across the street from Easy Motors. He laughed when he saw my shirt. "That's great. The readers will love it."

Frank didn't love it, though. When the receptionist announced my arrival, he stormed out of his office, his face the color of a ripe eggplant. "I told you not to come here harassing me again," he said.

"I brought a couple of friends I want you to meet." I turned to Mike and Sheila. "This is a reporter and a photographer from the *Houston Banner.*"

The color drained from Frank's face as he stared at the camera. Sheila took advantage of his momentary shock to snap off a couple of pictures before he barricaded himself in his office. "No comment!" he shouted through the closed door.

"You'd better leave," the receptionist said. "He's not going to come out as long as you're here." She smoothed her hair and smiled, showing all her teeth. "Before you go, would you take my picture?"

We retreated outside to the street corner, where Sheila took a few shots of me holding a sign I'd made that read Give Phoebe Her Car. As people stopped for the light, I handed out copies of the letter I'd sent to the paper to anybody who'd take one. People honked their horns and waved, and pretty soon a crowd had gathered. The manager of the Dairy Freeze on the opposite corner sent me a free soda and said I was good for business. Half a dozen workers from the car wash down the street gave me a sun visor and posed holding my sign.

A Channel Two news van pulled up and a perky blond reporter interviewed me. I gave her one of my letters, and recited my tale of woe. This celebrity business was actually kind of fun. Why had I been so worried about embarrassing myself? I was doing great.

A black Lexus pulled even with the curb and I offered the driver a copy of my letter. The smoked-glass window slid down and Steve gaped at me. "Phoebe, what are you doing?"

The Channel Two reporter stuck her microphone in Steve's face. "What do you think of Ms. Frame's campaign to receive fair treatment from Easy Motors?" she asked.

"I think she's crazy." He glared at me.

"This is my ex-husband, Steve Frame," I said to the camera. "He's the man who left me without a decent car to drive, and without enough money to buy a new one."

A chorus of boos issued from my fan club, which consisted mainly of six Mexican car-wash workers and two winos who had wandered over to see what all the excitement was about. Steve shut his window and sped away, burning rubber.

From time to time, Frank looked out the front door of Easy Motors and scowled for the camera. The crowd hissed and shouted obscenities in English and Spanish. At one point, we even had people doing the wave, and chanting, "Give Phoebe her car." Any minute now, I expected someone to start up a chorus of "We shall overcome."

By twelve-thirty, I'd given away all my letters, and the car-wash workers had to get back to work. The news van packed up and left and the winos wandered away in search of a better party. Mike shook my hand. "Great story, Phoebe. I hope it gets you your car."

"Thanks, Mike. I appreciate your help."

I was crossing the street toward the bus stop when a black pickup pulled up alongside me. The window slid down and Jeff grinned at me. "Want a ride?"

I couldn't think of a good reason to say no, so I opened the door and climbed in. To tell you the truth, I was glad to see him. The office had been a dull place without him around.

His week away hadn't dimmed his charm or dulled his looks. He had a healthy tan and sun had highlighted his dark hair. Instead of slacks and button-down shirt, he wore jeans and a T-shirt, and he hadn't bothered to shave. Looking at him made me weak in the knees. It ought to be against the law for a man to look that good.

"What are you doing in this neighborhood?" I asked, trying to distract myself from my decidedly impure thoughts.

"I was out running some errands and heard about you on the radio, so I decided to drive over and see for myself."

"You missed all the excitement." I grinned. "Channel Two was here."

"Think it'll help you get your car back?"

I shrugged. "I figure it couldn't hurt." I realized we weren't headed toward my house. I turned toward him. "Where are we going?"

"It's after lunch. I thought you might be hungry."

We ended up at an icehouse on Telephone Road, one of those places with a gravel parking lot and garage-door sides that roll up to let the breezes blow in. The air smelled of hot pavement, cigarettes and smoke from the barrel barbecue cookers lined up six abreast out back. Conjunto music blared from the jukebox and two old men in cowboy boots, faded jeans and tank tops played pool for quarters under a whirring ceiling fan.

We ordered paper plates piled with smoked brisket, beans and coleslaw, and sweating long-neck bottles of beer. We ate at a wooden picnic table in the shade of a spreading live oak, sitting on top of the table with our plates beside us, our feet propped on the bench.

We didn't say much while we ate, just enjoyed the smoky nirvana of perfectly cooked brisket and peppery sauce, washed down with beer so cold it made the muscles at the back of my jaw ache. I was still flushed from the thrill of the morning, of my temporary celebrity and the feeling that, for once, I'd gotten the best of a man who had tried to take advantage of me. I didn't have my car yet, but I'd made a good start. At least I'd gotten someone to listen to me and take me seriously.

Jeff drained his beer bottle and tossed it toward an old oil drum that served as a trash can. He leaned back on his hands and looked at me for a long while, saying nothing.

"What? Do I have barbecue sauce smeared on my face?" I brushed my cheek, but felt nothing.

The corners of his mouth lifted in the beginnings of a smile. He really did have great lips. Lips I couldn't look at without thinking of kissing him. "What?" I demanded again.

"Just admiring the view," he said. "You're a very pretty woman, Phoebe Frame."

I gave him a thoughtful look. "Your middle name isn't Eddie, is it?"

"No. It's Wayne." He frowned. "Why?"

"No reason." I started to get off the table, to put a little more distance between his too sexy good looks and honey-smooth voice, but he grabbed my hand and pulled me back. "I see you still have the ring." He stroked the jewel with his thumb.

"Steve is still trying to get it. He had his lawyer send me a letter offering four thousand dollars if I'd give it up."

He whistled. "That's a pretty good chunk of change."

I jerked my hand away from him. "It's not about the money."

He looked puzzled. "The ring means that much to you?
"It's a nice ring."
He sat forward, elbows on his knees. "You could buy a nice one to replace it with the money."
I knew what he was too polite to ask. He wanted to know why I wanted a ring that my ex-husband had given me. Why did I still want that tie to Steve?
I didn't know how to answer that question. Maybe I wanted the ring because it represented the good years of my marriage, when Steve and I had been in love. For that one brief time in my life, the future had looked full of promise. It wasn't wrong to want to hold on to that, was it?
When I didn't say anything, Jeff changed the subject. "Go out with me this evening. We could go dancing."
I think I would have enjoyed dancing with Jeff, swaying arm in arm to something soft and sultry. I shook off the fantasy and straightened my shoulders. "I can't. I have to work."
"Work? It's Saturday."
"Yeah, and I have a dozen charts to transcribe for Patterson." I shrugged. "Besides, I could use the overtime to pay for all those copies of my letter I handed out today."
"I don't like the idea of you alone there with Patterson."
"I'll be all right. If I'm lucky, he won't even show up."
He slid off the table and pulled out his keys. "I tell you what, I'll come with you."
"Don't be ridiculous." I stepped back, alarmed. "I don't need a baby-sitter." I also didn't need the distraction of thinking about the last time we'd been alone in that office.
"I won't distract you. I have some work of my own I need to do."
"Jeff, I really don't think that's a good idea. Especially after last time." There. I'd said it. Or at least let him know that I hadn't forgotten.
He grinned. "We could try the lab this time. Or the doctor's

office. That's a big desk he has." He waggled his eyebrows suggestively.

I burst out laughing, shaking my head. "Jeff, no! I really do have to work."

He took my elbow and steered me toward the truck. "Fine. I promise to let you get your work done if you promise to let me come with you."

"And if I don't let you?"

He slid his hand down my back, sending instant heat to every erogenous zone on my body. "I promise to do my damnedest to make you forget anything having to do with work."

I swallowed. This was a choice? "I have to work," I said weakly.

He squeezed my bottom, making me jump. "Great. We'll both work now." He unlocked his truck and opened the door for me. As I climbed into the cab, his hand brushed my bottom again. "But I promise we'll play later," he whispered, his breath tickling the back of my neck and making me wish my common sense would take a vacation. Far away. At least until I'd gotten Jeff out of my system. Like say, maybe in the next ten years?

DESPITE HIS SUGGESTIVE TEASING, Jeff was a man of his word and he left me alone in my workroom once we reached the office. I started in on my stack of charts and he disappeared into another part of the office, doing who knows what.

The longer I worked, the more annoyed I became with Patterson. Compiling all these chart notes was just busywork, the equivalent of being made to write "I will not shun the doctor's advances" five hundred times on the blackboard. I doubted he'd even use the information in his presentation.

This was the first time Patterson had been asked to speak at the conference, and you'd have thought he'd been asked to star in his own daytime talk show. The most favored patients got a blow-by-blow account of his invitation to speak, and the rest of us heard about it almost hourly. He couldn't return calls just now because he was working on his talk. He couldn't review a supply order because he had to research his talk. He couldn't interview a new transcriptionist because he was too busy preparing for his talk.

"The talk" had taken so much of his attention he'd almost—but not quite—slowed down his constant pursuit of the feminine form. At least he'd limited his advances toward me to those times when we were alone, with the occasional leer in my direction. But unless something happened to change him, he'd be back in top form after the conference.

An hour and a half into the afternoon's work, I took a much-deserved break and went looking for Jeff. I found him in the last place I'd expected him to be—Patterson's office.

In fact, he'd made himself right at home. He was sitting behind the doctor's bed-size desk, tapping away at Patterson's personal computer. "What are you doing in here?" I asked.

"Promise not to tell?" With one finger, he tapped out a string of letters and numbers and hit Enter.

"That depends." I perched on the edge of the desk. "Is it something interesting and too juicy to keep a secret?"

"Hardly." He hit another series of keys, then swiveled the doctor's high-back leather chair around to face me. "I'm snooping."

"You mean...hacking?"

"That's a crude term for it, but yes."

I grinned. "Find anything good?"

"I was hoping he might have kept a log of his conquests, or his Web browser would be full of naughty sites he'd visited, or I'd find a cache of secret love letters to some high-muckety-muck's wife." He shook his head. "But I didn't find anything but boring medical files and financial data."

"Patterson's a slime, but he's not dumb," I said.

He picked up a pencil and began turning it over and over in his hand. "He's arrogant. Arrogant people think they're too good to get caught, so they make stupid mistakes. You wouldn't believe the stuff I've found on people's computers."

"What do you do when you find out something naughty?"

He shrugged. "Nothing. It's none of my business. But for Patterson, I might make an exception."

I glanced over my shoulder, as if I half expected the good doctor himself to come bursting in. "What would you do if you found something dirty about him?" I asked.

"I'd use the information to blackmail him into leaving you alone."

His expression was all hard lines—jutting jaw, eyebrows knitted fiercely together. A true knight, risking, if not his life, then his reputation, to protect me. I was touched. And more than a little turned on.

"You'd do that for me?" I asked, the quaver in my voice betraying my emotions.

He looked away, a flush of red creeping up from his collar. "Yeah, well I didn't find anything, did I?" He leaned over and punched the power button. The screen image shrank to a pinpoint of light, then vanished.

He shoved up out of the chair and moved out from behind the desk. "Finished with your work?"

I shook my head. "Hardly." I stretched my arms over my head, arching my back. "I just needed a break."

He came up behind me and began massaging my neck. It felt so good, I almost groaned. The man had magic hands. Strong, but gentle. Every knot melted away at his expert touch. I sagged against him, eyes closed. "You could have a second career as a massage therapist."

"I don't do this for just anybody, you know." He slid his

hands over my shoulders, until they covered the tops of my breasts. My nipples stood at attention.

There are times when a conscience is more curse than convenience, and this was one of them. "Jeff..." I said in warning.

He took his hands from me and stepped back. "I know, I know. But I can't help wanting to touch you."

I looked at him, trying to see beyond the charming exterior to the man within. "Why? What does a young, good-looking guy with his own successful business see in an older, recently divorced woman who's overdrawn on all her credit cards and can't even get her car out of hock, much less her life in order?"

He grinned. "I find your modesty so charming." He shoved his hands in his pockets. "Seriously, you don't give yourself enough credit. When I look at you, I see a woman who's been dealt a bad hand but who's rising above all that. You haven't let the bad things make you bitter."

I crossed my legs primly. "I'm sure there are plenty of non-bitter women your own age out there."

"Yeah, but I have this thing for old women like you." He put his hands on the desktop, on either side of my thighs, trapping me. His chest brushed the tips of my breasts and he stared into my eyes. "I figure if I play my cards right, in a few years I can live off your social security and take advantage of all the senior-citizen specials at restaurants."

"You're making fun of me," I breathed.

"Uh-huh." He dipped his head and covered my mouth with his own, pressing his body more fully against mine.

I didn't want this to be happening, but I couldn't make it stop. I didn't know if Jeff was right for me, or what direction my life would take next, but, right now, none of that mattered up against the fact of this man touching me, calling forth sensations from my body that had been shoved aside or forgotten or maybe had never even existed before.

"Jeff," I whispered. I'd meant a protest, but it came out like an endearment.

"Phoebe." My name was soft on his lips, warm and breathy and heavy with meaning. My hands slid back, sending a stack of folders and a stethoscope sliding to the floor. He brought his hand around to my back to support me, and I threw my arms around him, silently telling all doubts and misgivings to take a hike.

"One of these days, we're going to have to try a bed," Jeff mumbled as he pushed me further back on the desk and fumbled with the snap of my jeans.

"There are eight other desks, four exam-room tables and a gurney in this office." I grinned at him as he found the catch on my bra and unhooked it. "It could be a while before we'll even need a bed."

"Should we try for them all tonight, or pace ourselves?"

"I'm betting you give out before I do." I grinned and tugged at the hem of his T-shirt.

"I don't know. A young stud like me might be too much for an old lady like you." He stripped off his shirt, and my smile was lost in a flood of desire, and not a little bit of triumph. This magnificent man wanted me. He didn't care if my breasts weren't as perky as they'd once been, or if I had more cottage cheese on my thighs than the average dairy case. He wanted to be with me. To love me.

I leaned back and struck a provocative pose. "Come here, big boy. Let's see if you can keep up."

It's no secret, forbidden pleasure is an aphrodisiac all its own. I suppose making love on the boss's desk is the equivalent of making out in your parents' car. It's naughty, there's a chance you might get caught, and that makes it that much more fun.

It isn't particularly comfortable, though, and by the third time some office gadget poked me in the rump, I was ready to cry uncle and suggest we head for a hotel. Jeff shoved the stapler out of the way and laughed. "I've got a better idea."

And that's how he ended up on the desk, giving me the ride of my life. That was so much fun, we tried the chair, which was quite a moving experience, once we discovered the rollers had no trouble traveling on carpet. I was all ready to give the gurney a go when Jeff admitted he needed a rest. "I'm vanquished," he said, wrapping his arms around me and pulling me to the carpet.

I rested my head on his chest and giggled. "What's so funny?" he asked.

"I have a confession to make."

"You mean...you're not a virgin?"

I pretended to punch him. "No, my confession is that I've never had so much fun making love."

He patted my shoulder. "Then I'd say you've got a lot of catching up to do. And as soon as I've recovered, I'll get back to making up for that deficit."

I kissed him long and hard, letting him know just how much I approved of that idea. One kiss led to another, and we were so wrapped up in the moment, we almost didn't hear footsteps approaching down the hall.

"What's that?" Jeff raised his head, listening.

"What's what?" I giggled, and tried to pull him down to my level once more.

He shoved up onto one elbow and looked toward the office door. "Someone's coming."

13

I HEARD IT THEN, TOO. Shoes thudding on the hall carpet, headed this way. "Oh, my God!"

Knocking heads and bumping elbows, we scrambled for our clothes. "We've got to get out of here!" Jeff whispered, eyes wild.

"In here." I grabbed his hand and dragged him toward the bathroom. He stopped long enough to shove the chair back into place and toss the stethoscope onto the desk. We pulled the door shut behind us just as Patterson strolled in.

Stifling a squeak of fright, I urged Jeff toward the shower stall. We stood behind the black vinyl shower curtain, clutching various articles of clothing about us. "What's he doing here?" Jeff croaked.

I shrugged, and strained my ears to listen. I heard desk drawers opening and closing, papers rattling, then a long silence.

"He must have left," Jeff whispered in my ear.

I nodded, still too afraid to move.

"Come on. I think the coast is cl—" Jeff had his hand on the curtain, about to pull it back, when the bathroom door opened and Patterson stepped in.

We froze, staring at each other in bug-eyed fear. I don't think I even breathed. Any minute now, Patterson would rip back that curtain and demand to know the meaning of this. I suppose I could have told him the plumbing wasn't working at my house and I'd decided to take a shower, but I didn't think he'd buy the part that Jeff was just trying to save water by joining me.

The curtain never moved. I heard the sound of a zipper, then the cascade of water into the toilet. Patterson whistled while he peed. I swear, does going to the bathroom make men that happy or are they just trying to distract themselves?

With this thought in mind, I made the mistake of looking at Jeff. He grinned and puffed his cheeks out, miming whistling. I clamped my teeth together, stifling laughter, and telegraphed threatening messages with my eyes. Inside me, laughter expanded like popping corn, threatening at any moment to explode.

At last, Patterson left us. We listened as his footsteps retreated, then waited through half a lifetime of silence before either of us moved. "I think he's really gone this time," Jeff whispered.

I nodded, feet still stuck to the bottom of the tub.

"Why don't I get dressed and go check? If I run into him, I can always tell him I was checking the network."

I nodded again. Jeff pulled his shirt over his head, then nodded toward my hand. "Could I have my briefs, or are you saving them for a souvenir?"

I looked down and saw that I had mashed Jeff's briefs into a golf-ball-size wad. "Sorry." I handed them over and pawed through the other clothes in my arms. "If I have your briefs, where are my panties?"

We couldn't locate them, so I ended up putting on my jeans without underwear. It felt naughty and sexy, and I prayed I wouldn't get anything caught in my zipper next time I went to the bathroom.

Jeff left and I finished dressing. Sometime between pulling on my jeans and fastening the strap of my sandals, the reality of my situation hit me. If Patterson had walked in even five minutes earlier, he would have caught me rolling around naked on the floor of his office with a man who was technically a co-worker. I'd risked my job and my reputation, and for what? For an hour or so of bliss with a man who couldn't be serious for more than a few minutes without cracking a joke?

I sagged against the bathroom sink, my buoyant mood vanished. I had to face facts: Jeff was a great guy. A lot of fun to be with. But he was not ready to settle down and start raising a family. And I was.

"All clear." He stuck his head around the corner of the bathroom. "Oh, and I found these." He held up a pair of pink cotton panties.

I grabbed the underwear and stuffed it into my pocket. "Where were they?"

His grin widened. "Hanging from the top of the ficus plant in the corner. I guess you threw them there in all the, um, excitement." He pulled me close and nuzzled my neck. "Speaking of which...want to try out the gurney?"

I shook my head and gently pushed him away. "I think I'd better go home now."

"Good idea. We can try out your bed."

"I'm going home alone."

"Alone?" He looked surprised.

I nodded. "I've had enough excitement for one night. I need a little time alone to try to figure things out."

He shook his head. "You think too much. Everything doesn't have to be analyzed, you know."

"Most of the mistakes I've made in my life have come from not thinking enough. I don't want this to be like that."

"This? You mean us?"

I nodded. "Yeah, us." I brushed back my hair and tried not to look as upset as I felt. "You're fun to be with, Jeff. You make me feel good. But I'm not sure if that's what I need to be doing right now."

"You said yourself you hadn't had enough fun before."

"Not enough fun in bed." I glanced at the jumbled desktop. "Or out of it." I straightened my shoulders and tried to look stern. "Common sense goes out the window when I'm around you. I'm not sure that's a good thing."

"I can be sensible, Phoebe. Give me a chance."

A chance to do what? Screw up my heart, and maybe my future? I ducked under his arm and out the door. "Go home and rest," I called over my shoulder. "I'll see you Monday."

He didn't answer right away. I was almost to the end of the hall when he called out, "Good night, Scarlett."

I whirled around. "Scarlett?"

He shrugged. "Scarlett O'Hara. Isn't she the one who said 'I'll think about it tomorrow'?"

"I thought she said 'fiddle-dee-dee' and 'I'll never go hungry again.'"

"That, too." He straightened. "Good night, Phoebe. I'll let you run away from me this time, but one of these days I won't let you off so easily."

I fluttered my fingers at him. "Fiddle-dee-dee." Then I hurried away, heart pounding. Damn right I was running. But I was also leaving a little bit of myself behind, soaked into Jeff's skin and tucked in next to his heart.

I WOULD HAVE PREFERRED to stay home the next day and mope and eat chocolate, but I'd promised Darla I'd go to the final game of Tony's big bowling tournament and help cheer for Tony.

"So, Phoebe, are you ready to cheer our boys on to victory?" Darla, in pink capri pants and a green-and-white T-shirt that read Go Ace Trucking Tigers across the front, hurried over to me when I arrived at the bowling alley. "Here, you'll need these." She handed me a pair of green-and-white plastic pom-poms.

"Cheerleading? For bowlers?"

"Hey, if football and basketball can have cheerleaders, why not bowling?" Tony winked at Darla. "Besides, we've got the best-looking supporters in this place."

Which wasn't saying much, considering this was not exactly a bunch of highly trained athletes. From the number of pot bellies within view, I'd say this crowd's idea of weight lifting was to hoist a few schooners of beer.

I shook the pom-poms. "I always wanted to be a cheerleader."

"Well, now's your chance." Darla raised her arms over her head. "Give me a *T!* Give me an *I!*"

"What's she doing?"

A familiar masculine voice sent a shiver down my spine. I turned and found Jeff standing behind me. "Hi," I said. "I didn't know you bowled."

"I haven't tried it in years."

"Then what are you doing here?"

"Darla invited me." He nodded toward my friend, who was finishing up her cheer by executing the splits. "Apparently this tournament is a really big deal."

"Apparently." I turned back around so he couldn't read the expression on my face. The smell of him was still on my skin and the memory of our lovemaking glowed technicolor bright in my brain. Now probably wasn't the best time to be making objective decisions about our relationship.

Jeff came around the bench and sat next to me. "Does it bother you that I'm here?"

I assumed what I hoped was a casual expression. "No. Why should it bother me?"

"You don't look too happy to see me."

"I'm just nervous," I said. "About the game. Why are you here? You don't really know Darla or Tony that well."

He grinned and laid his hand along the back of the bench,

his fingers almost, but not quite touching me. "That's easy. Darla told me you were going to be here."

"So you came here because of me? Why?" I was a little annoyed at the way my heart sped up at the thought. What happened to being an independent woman, relying on myself, not needing others' approval?

"I thought it would be good for us to see each other outside of work. Get to know each other better."

On some levels, we couldn't get to know each other any better than we already had at the office...in my workroom...on Patterson's desk...

"Why are you blushing?" He squeezed my shoulder and scooted closer. "Are you thinking naughty thoughts about me?"

I looked away, at a man warming up to bowl his first frame. "I—I'm embarrassed for that man," I said. "Someone should tell him double-knit slacks don't do anything for him."

We watched the bowlers for a while, saying nothing. Bowling is like a kind of dance, as if bulls or elephants or some other creature not made for dancing suddenly decided to try out a few steps. Every bowler has his or her own style, the way they dip down to deliver the ball, the way they kick their foot out at the end of their delivery.

After a while, though, I noticed the bowlers weren't the only ones getting physical. Jeff had moved his hand over until his fingers were resting on my shoulder. His touch was light at first, just a gentle stroking. Then he began caressing, kneading my shoulder. Tingles of sensation radiated across my back and down my spine. I squirmed on the hard plastic bench. "Will you stop that?" I snapped.

"Stop what?" He assumed a patently fake expression of innocence.

"Pawing me." I scooted away from him.

"Sorry." He looked sheepish and took his hand away. "I just like the way you feel."

What was I supposed to say to that? I got up and joined Darla on the sidelines. She was waving her pom-poms and bouncing on her toes. I ought to mention that Darla really was a cheerleader in high school, whereas I was too shy to try out.

"Go, Tony!" she yelled. "Bowl a strike, baby!"

Tony turned to grin at her and she blew him a kiss.

"Why did you invite Jeff?" I asked.

She lowered her pom-poms and shrugged. "I thought if you saw him outside of work, in a social setting, you might change your mind about him."

"Why would you think that?"

"He's a nice guy, Phoebe."

"How do you know that?"

"I called the office the other day but you were out delivering memos to other offices or something. So Jeff and I ended up talking for quite a while." She put her hand on my shoulder. "You ought to give him a chance."

I hugged my arms across my chest. "I know he's a nice guy. He's just not right for me."

She put her hands on her hips. "Why do you say that? And don't say he's too young."

"But he is too young. We're at different places in our lives. He's still sowing his wild oats. I'm ready to settle down."

"What's wrong with sowing wild oats? You've been settled down for twelve years. Maybe it's time to try something else."

"I'm going to the snack bar. Do either of you ladies want anything?" Jeff came up behind us. I blushed, wondering if he'd heard any of our conversation.

Darla smiled at him. "No thanks, Jeff. I'm fine."

"What about you, Phoebe?"

"I'll come with you." I followed him to the snack bar,

where he ordered a beer for himself and a Diet Coke for me. He didn't say a word to me until we were on our way back to our seats.

"Phoebe—" he began.

Just then, two small, screaming boys raced past, almost knocking us backward. Jeff swore as half his beer sloshed onto the floor, then reached out one hand to steady me. "You okay?"

"Yeah." I laughed and looked after the running children. "I don't think they ever saw us."

He frowned. "Parents shouldn't let kids run wild like that."

I shrugged. "Oh, they're just being kids."

"They're just being brats."

I stared at him, startled by his reaction. "You don't like children?"

"Oh, I hear they're quite good fried."

"Jeff!"

He laughed. "It's just a joke, Phoebe."

He retrieved a handful of napkins from a dispenser and handed me half. "Do you ever think about having children?" I asked as I mopped soda from my arm.

He shrugged. "Not really."

"Why not?"

"I just haven't thought about it much."

He gave me a funny look and I decided I'd better back off. Have you ever gotten lost in a strange city and ended up in a bad neighborhood? You know that feeling you get in the pit of your stomach—equal parts fear and self-loathing because, after all, you got yourself into this? If you'd paid attention or read the map, you wouldn't be here.

That's the way I felt with Jeff. I had told myself early on not to get too attached to him. That we weren't right for each other. And now that he was proving my prediction true, all I could think was that it was too late. I wasn't going to get out of this without getting hurt.

"What about you?" he asked. "Why don't you have any children? Or is that question too personal?"

I looked away. "Steve didn't want them."

"But I thought... isn't his fiancée pregnant?"

Fiancée. The word sounded strange. It's hard to think of your ex-husband as having a fiancée. "Yeah."

"I'm not sure I understand," Jeff said.

"Join the club."

We didn't say anything else as we made our way back to our seats and pretended to watch the tournament. I know I wasn't really paying attention to the bowlers and I could feel Jeff's eyes on me. Maybe I never should have brought up the kid thing. But wasn't it better to know now, before I got in any deeper?

"Isn't it terrific?" Darla bounced over to us, eyes shining.

"Isn't what terrific?" I asked.

"The tournament. The Tigers only need thirty points to win. And Tony's up next."

I watched with renewed interest as Tony retrieved his bowling ball and readied himself. He brought the ball to his chest and stared down the lane at the pins like a general staring down opposing forces. A hush fell over the crowd as Tony brought the ball back in a smooth arc and began his approach. His feet were practically soundless as he took three strides forward and released the ball. It barreled down the lane, arcing toward the pins, a purple blur reflected in the waxed wood of the lane.

The pins exploded up and outward with a tremendous crash, the sound of their falling drowned out by the cheers of Tony's teammates. Darla jumped up and down and waved her pom-poms wildly.

"He only needs to bowl two more strikes and they win," she squealed.

"Is he that good?" I never thought a bowling tournament could be so exciting, but here I was, on my feet, palms sweating as Tony readied his next shot.

Darla shot me a scolding look. "Of course he's that good. He's the best player on the team."

"Sorry." But she didn't even hear me over the roar of the crowd as Tony bowled his second strike.

Darla's not one to hold a grudge, however, and, as Tony set up for his third shot, she came over and wrapped her arms around me. "I can't look," she whispered, and buried her head in my shoulder.

Tony brought the ball up to his chest, then back in a fluid movement. He reminded me of a slow-motion film as he stepped forward, then launched the ball. I leaned forward with him, urging the ball forward...forward...forward.

The ball struck the pins and they tumbled down, rolling and spinning away. The crowd gasped as one pin wobbled like a drunk trying to regain his balance. Over, then up. Over, then up. Around, around, around....

When it fell, Tony's teammates surrounded him, pounding his back and shouting. Darla squeezed me tight. "He did it! He did it! He won the tournament."

I grabbed both her hands and squeezed them. Tony came up and threw his arms around both of us. "Congratulations," I told him.

"Come on," he said. "We're all going over to Pizza Palace to celebrate. I'll buy you a drink."

"I'll buy you one, too." Darla glanced around. "Where's Jeff? We should ask him to go."

I looked over to the bench where we had been sitting, but it was empty. Jeff wasn't with the bowlers celebrating their victory, or over by the snack bar. "Maybe he's in the men's room," I said.

We finally sent Tony into the men's room to check, but he came back shaking his head. "He's not in there." We went outside then, but his car wasn't in the parking lot, either.

"Did he just leave?" Darla asked. "Without saying goodbye?" She looked at me. "Did you two argue about something?"

"No...well, not really."

"Phoebe, what did you say to him?"

"Darla, honey, let it drop." Tony put his arm around her shoulders. "Let's go have pizza and have a good time. Maybe the guy wasn't feeling well. Or maybe he had someplace else he had to be."

Or maybe all the talk about children had put him in a bad mood. It had put me in a bad mood, too, but I didn't have the choice of going home and sulking. I had to go with my friends and pretend to have a good time.

Why is it, just when I think I've got my life figured out, someone comes along and throws a big monkey wrench in it? It's enough to make a woman want to join a convent.

14

I DIDN'T SEE JEFF for the next week. I tried calling his office and got his answering service. "Uh, just tell him Phoebe called," I muttered and hung up.

Well. I didn't know whether to be pissed off that he was avoiding me or worried that I'd ticked him off somehow. Maybe he was just tired of me playing hard to get.

Not that I'd set out to play exactly, but I hadn't thrown myself into his arms, either.

Or maybe he was just tired of me. The way Steve had grown tired of me.

Ugh. Jeff was not Steve. And I wasn't doing anyone any good sitting here trying to second-guess his motives. Fine, next time I saw Jeff we'd have it out. I'd tell him I was ready to start thinking about maybe having a relationship with him, but he was going to have to be patient.

After all, Mama always said good things were worth waiting for. Surely I was a good thing for Jeff.

Wasn't I?

In any case, while I waited for Jeff to return my call, or at least show up at the office, I had plenty of things to occupy my mind, what with all the extra work Patterson was giving me and my repeated attempts to get Easy Motors to release my car. I'd taken to bombarding various government agencies with complaint letters, hoping to get some results, but so far, nothing was happening.

I'd searched the paper every day for the article Mike Dawson was supposed to write, but it hadn't shown up, either. To tell you the truth, I was getting discouraged.

Of course, work and the situation with my car didn't mean I didn't think about Jeff. I thought about him a lot. When he didn't return my call after a day and a half, I called his office again. This time I reached a secretary, who told me he was out of town. I hung up before she asked my name. I felt as though I was in high school again, calling boys and hanging up because I was too scared to talk to them.

I planned to spend that Saturday cleaning house and listing all the reasons why I should calm down and risk a little romance with Jeff. I planned to work up the perfect speech to announce my feelings to him—as soon as I could figure out what those feelings were.

But that's what happens when you make plans. You're just asking for someone to come along and blow them all to hell.

In this case, the person who came along was Darla, so I couldn't complain. Who wants to dust and clean toilets anyway?

Darla offered plenty of distraction. She burst into the house with a dozen Krispy Kreme doughnuts in one hand and a hefty shopping bag in the other. "Look!" She thrust the box of doughnuts into my chest, then shoved her hand under my nose, displaying a diamond the size of a large chocolate chip. "Isn't it gorgeous? Tony gave it to me last night when he popped the question."

It was gorgeous, in the way only a big, gaudy hunk of precious stone can be. "Congratulations!" I squealed, and hugged her. To tell you the truth, I'd had my doubts about Tony ever making an honest woman of Darla. After all, they'd been dating six years. I was thrilled he'd finally done right by my friend.

We celebrated with a fresh pot of coffee and half the doughnuts. "So, have you set a date?" I asked.

"Sometime in November. Before the holidays. But we're not really sure." She reached under the table and drew out the shopping bag. "That's another reason I came over here. I need your help."

She upended the bag and magazines slid across the tabletop. *Bride's, Modern Bride, Bridal Guide, Wedding Planner, Wonderful Weddings.* "What is all this?" I asked.

"I've been waiting for years for this, but now that it's here, I don't know what to do." She picked up a magazine and flipped through it. "I have to plan a wedding. But first I have to decide what kind of wedding I want." She shoved a magazine toward me. "Look. This couple got married in a vineyard. The reception was a wine tasting." She tossed another issue toward me. "This one has a story about a couple who got married at a zoo."

She slumped forward, chin in her hands. "It's not enough to just get married. Weddings have themes these days. I need you to help me decide on a theme."

I looked at a picture of a smiling bride and groom posing next to an elephant. The elephant had a wreath of magnolia blossoms perched between its enormous ears. "I think I'd stay away from anything to do with animals." I shoved the magazine aside. "What do you want to do?"

"All kinds of things. The problem is, I've had too much time to think about this. When you're nineteen and get married, you've probably only been fantasizing about it ten years or so. You go for the white gown, the black tux, the church and the orange blossoms. Your mom cries. Your dad is nervous. The photographer takes forever."

That was my wedding in a nutshell. My mom fluttered around like a crazed moth, my dad chewed his fingernails until they bled and Steve locked his keys in his car and had to call a locksmith to get his tux out of the back seat. The preacher called me Penelope when he introduced us to the congregation and the best man made a lewd comment just as Steve was taking off my garter, so the wedding picture showed me with my eyes bugged out and my mouth open so wide you can see my tonsils.

"I've had too much time," Darla continued. "I'm thirty-three. I've had twenty-six years to think about this, at least. One minute, I want a traditional church wedding. Then I think a wedding on a cruise ship would be nice. Or what about a wedding in a foreign country, Jamaica or the Bahamas? I can't decide."

"What does Tony want?"

She snorted. "He wants what every man wants. He wants to elope. Ten minutes in the judge's office and you're done. I told him he could forget that idea. I want a real wedding. One I'll remember."

I smiled. "You really don't remember, you know. You sort of float around in a daze the whole day. The next morning, you wake up and look at the gold band on your finger and the man in bed next to you and you realize it really did happen. But you don't remember it."

Those magical blissful moments have all the staying power of the soap bubbles they blow at weddings now instead of tossing rice. It's a million other moments in marriage that stick in your head: the night he came home late and refused to tell you where he'd been. The fight you had when he insulted your mother. The way his face looked when he told you he didn't love you anymore.

"At least I'll have a video." Darla pushed the pile of magazines aside. "I can't think. I'm too excited to know what I want. Let's talk about something else." She folded her hands in front of her and looked at me expectantly. "So how's Jeff?"

"Jeff?" I cleared my throat and tried to sound less guilty. "He's fine. I guess."

I got up and poured more coffee. Maybe instead of brooding about Jeff on my own, I should talk to somebody about it. Darla had given me good advice about things before. "About Jeff..." I began.

She tore her gaze away from her ring. "He's coming to the clinic Halloween party, isn't he? Have you decided on a costume, yet?"

I dropped into a chair. "I hadn't really thought about it." Every year, the Central Care Network Clinic gave a huge Halloween party. Everyone came in costume, there was great food and drink and door prizes. It's one of the few things they did for employees that was genuinely fun—at Christmas, we would get an ornament with a picture of the clinic on it. This was supposed to make us feel appreciated?

"I'm not sure I want to go this year," I said. The prospect of trying to avoid both Jeff and Patterson while we were all in costume didn't appeal to me for some reason.

"Don't be silly! You have to go. If you don't go, you don't get your full share of employee benefits." She grinned. "Besides, it's your one chance to really wow everybody with a dynamite costume. So what do you think you'll go as?"

I shrugged. "I guess I could pull out the witch costume I wore last year." The pointed hat had gotten crushed when a pumpkin from the neurosurgeon's office had sat on it, but I could probably straighten it out.

"Don't be ridiculous. You should go as something you've always wanted to be. As a way of empowering yourself."

"A Halloween costume can be empowering?"

"Absolutely. It's a kind of visualization. I read an article about it in the dentist's office last month. Now come on, what's your fantasy?"

I thought a moment. "I guess what I want most is to be a strong, powerful woman who doesn't take shit from anybody. But how are you going to get a costume out of that?"

Darla looked thoughtful. "What about sexy?"

I squirmed. "Well, yeah, I want to be sexy, too. I want to be the kind of woman who has men worshiping at my feet. But no costume is going to do that for me."

A smile spread across her face. "Actually, I think I've got the perfect costume for you."

"What?"

"Oh, I'm not going to tell you now." Her grin was evil. "Leave everything to me. You're going to love it!"

Monday morning, I arrived at the office to find a picture of me cut from the paper and taped to the wall in the employee break room at the clinic. There I was, wearing my Lemon T-shirt, holding a sign that read Give Phoebe Her Car. The Easy Motors sign loomed behind me and I thought I could just make out Frank's face scowling at the entrance to the dealer's office.

"Phoebe, you're famous," Michelle said as she poured coffee. "You made the front page of the metro section."

I read the article taped below the picture. Mike Dawson had finally come through for me. He'd done a great job, too, portraying me as a crusading woman who was tired of being taken advantage of. He even got in a dig about Steve. "While Frame's ex drives a Lexus, she was left with a twelve-year-old car that promptly died six months after their divorce."

I grinned. Later, maybe I'd highlight that section of the article and mail a copy to Steve's office.

"Have you seen Albert's hat?" Barb came into the break room, the skeleton in her arms. "I thought I left it on the top shelf of the supply closet last year, but it's not there."

"I think I saw it in the cabinet over the refrigerator," Michelle said.

Barb leaned Albert against the counter and dragged a step stool over to the refrigerator. "Here it is." She waved the black-and-orange ball cap in triumph. "Oh, and here's the pumpkin lights for around the reception desk."

"Is it time to decorate already?" I asked. Halloween was...I glanced at the calendar. Only two weeks away. Yikes!

"Here, why don't you dress up your workroom?" Barb tossed a ball of spider webbing at me. "We've got rubber spiders, too."

"Just don't put the candy out yet," Michelle said. "Last year I gained five pounds and could hardly fit into my costume."

Barb looked down her nose at Michelle. "If that Elvira dress wasn't so tight, you wouldn't have that problem."

"Your bunch-of-grapes costume didn't hide anything any better than my Elvira outfit."

Barb blushed. "I was fine until some wise guy decided to pop my balloons."

Poor Barb. I'd thought her idea to tape purple balloons all over her body to resemble a bunch of grapes had been a good one, until the balloons had popped and she'd been left standing there in a purple leotard with a grape-leaf hat.

"What are you coming as this year, Phoebe?" Michelle asked.

"I don't know."

"Come on," Barb said. "You can tell us."

"Honest. I don't know. Darla's planning something for me. It'll be a surprise."

"Can somebody tell me where I'm supposed to put this?" Jeff stood in the doorway, an enormous pumpkin in his arms.

I stared at him. "What are you doing here?" I asked. *And why didn't you call me as soon as you got back in town?*

"Ms. Lee wants me to make some modifications to the system."

So much for thinking he'd come to see me. I turned away, hoping my disappointment didn't show on my face.

"Just put the pumpkin over here in the sink," Barb said. "We still have to carve it."

"Why don't you get Dr. Patterson to do it?" Michelle said. "He ought to be good with a scalpel."

"I asked him, but he said he's too busy writing his talk."

"You're looking very nice this morning, Phoebe."

How is it the way one particular man says your name can make your insides turn to mush? Nobody else acted as though they noticed anything, but when Jeff said my name, all I could think of was those moments in his arms on Patterson's desk. "Uh...thank you," I squeaked.

"Are you coming to the Halloween party?" he asked.

"Y—yes. Are you?"

He smiled, a slow, seductive smile that made my temperature go up five degrees. "Oh, I wouldn't miss it."

"She won't tell us what her costume is," Barb said. "It's a secret."

"I don't know what it is," I protested. "Darla's putting it together for me."

"You could come as a protester and wear your T-shirt." He pointed to my picture on the wall. "Have you heard from Easy Motors?"

"Not yet. But I'm going to keep after them."

"Good for you." Michelle stood and tossed her napkin into the trash. "Don't let them walk all over you."

"What is everyone doing in here?" Joan Lee appeared in the doorway. "We have work to do."

"I just came in to get the Halloween decorations." Barb put the hat on Albert and looped the pumpkin lights around his neck.

"Do the decorations later. We have patients to take care of." With that, she turned and stalked out of the room.

"Yes, Miss Lee." Jeff's voice was a perfect mimic of every robotic classroom reply I'd ever heard, but his face was perfectly solemn. He picked up Albert and marched him toward the door. "I'll get right on it."

I took this as my cue to head back to my cubby. So much for celebrity. It doesn't last, but then, what good thing does?

I'd just booted up my computer when Jeff came into my cave. "I need to look at a few things on the system," he said, taking a seat at the other terminal.

I swiveled my chair to face him. Jeff always looked at me when we were together, one of the things about him I found most flattering. Today, he kept his eyes averted. "We need to talk," I said.

"About what?" He typed in a string of letters and symbols, still not looking at me. Okay, I was getting annoyed. Glare at me, shout at me, make faces at me, but do not ignore me.

I leaned over and hit the off button on his monitor.

"What the h—" He looked at me then, anger sparking in his eyes. "Why did you do that?"

"Why did you run out before the end of the bowling tournament?"

He shrugged, and assumed that macho-guy, too-cool-for-anything-to-upset-me expression. Which was stupid because it told me he was upset. "It was time for me to leave."

"What's that supposed to mean?"

He shook his head and turned back to the computer to switch the monitor back on.

I reached over and switched it off again.

When he glared at me, I glared right back. "Try that again and I'll unplug it," I said.

He sat back in his chair, arms crossed over his chest, and continued to scowl at me. Not talking. As if I was going to let him get away with that.

"Look," I said. "I'm not a mind reader. If I said something that upset you, you'd better tell me."

"You've been saying things to me for weeks. I guess that day I was finally ready to hear."

And this was man-code for what? "What are you talking about?"

He uncrossed his arms and sat up straighter. "You've been telling me you didn't want to get involved with me, but I never believed it before that day at the bowling alley."

And he believed it now? Just when I'd changed my mind? Men! You couldn't depend on them. "I don't know what you're talking about. What happened at the bowling alley?"

"When we were talking about your ex. Steve. And his fiancée. I understood then that the reason you didn't want to go out with me was that you're still in love with him."

Obviously, this was some kind of nightmare. Or I'd heard wrong. Jeff couldn't possibly have accused me of still being in love with my ex. The lying jerk who'd dumped me in the name of personal freedom and had scarcely waited for the ink on the change-of-address forms to dry before he'd taken up with a younger, perkier woman.

"You think I'm carrying the torch for Steve?"

Jeff nodded.

I stood, too agitated to sit still. "That's ridiculous. I can't stand Steve's guts. I ought to send Tami flowers and thank her for taking him off my hands."

He shifted in his chair, confusion glazing his eyes. "Do you mean that?"

"Of course I mean it." I shuddered. Lately, I'd spent more than a little time asking myself what I'd ever seen in Steve Frame.

Jeff frowned. "You acted so odd when we were talking about Steve having a kid. I assumed that meant you were jealous of him and Tami."

"I'm pissed off that he spent all those years refusing to even discuss having children with me and now he's walking around like a candidate for father of the year. Makes me sick."

Jeff's next move surprised me. He reached out and grabbed both my hands. "Then why won't you go out with me? Don't say it's the age difference, because that's a bunch of bull. Don't say you're trying to get your life together, because I can help you with that."

I nodded. His hands felt nice around mine. Strong and warm. "Okay."

He blinked. "Okay what?"

"Okay, I won't say any of those things."

"Then what will you say?"

I smiled. "I'll go out with you."

"When?"

"Whenever you like."

He pulled me toward him. Giggling, I half fell, half sat in his lap. We kissed, a sweet, searing meeting of our lips that made me aware of how much I'd missed him.

"Hrrrmph!"

For a small woman, Joan Lee can clear her throat quite loudly. We flew apart and stared at the office manager, who fixed us with a freezing gaze. "Mr. Fischer, you are here to adjust the transcription program, not the transcriptionist," she said.

I scrambled to my feet and smoothed my dress, cursing the rush of blood to my face. "Phoebe, you are to conduct yourself in a more professional manner," Joan said.

"Of course." I turned to my monitor, hiding a satisfied grin. I felt giddy, and a little afraid, too. I'd just agreed to go on a real date with my handsome young stud. What kind of crazy thing would I do next?

15

"I'M HUNGRY. Let's get something to eat."

I looked up from my computer at six o'clock that evening to find Jeff standing over me. "Now?" I said.

"You promised me a date. I figure I'd better collect on that promise before you change your mind."

"Why would I change my mind?" I adopted a teasing tone.

"You're a woman. That's what women do."

I laughed and switched off my monitor. "That's right. So you'd better watch your step." Already my skin was tingling at the thought of the evening ahead. A whole evening with the magic man here. I wish I'd taken my vitamins. I had a feeling I might need them.

We drove to a Mexican food place and ordered cheese enchiladas. He smiled at me while the waitress arranged our food on the table. I fidgeted in the booth across from him. Sure, we'd eaten together before, but that had been as friends. This was...something different. I wanted the evening to turn out well, but I was wary of reading too much into it.

When the waitress was gone, he said, "I can't believe this is our first real date. It seems like I've known you for months."

I prodded my enchiladas with a fork. "Yeah, but all those times at the office weren't real dates."

"Come on, you liked it as much as I did."

I shrugged. "I never said I didn't. It's just..."

"Just what?"

I laid aside my fork and met his gaze. "I'm not sure what

kind of relationship we have going here. Are you really interested in me, or is it just a physical thing?"

"I'm really interested in you." The way he said the words, as if he was absolutely positive, sent an excited tremble through me.

"Then tell me about yourself," I said. "Not the stuff I know from the office, about your business and stuff, but about you."

He took a sip of beer. "All right. I'm the youngest of four children, the only boy." He grinned. "Maybe that's why I like women. Strong women." He scooped up a forkful of enchilada. "I'm ambitious. I like to ski. I like alternative rock and kung fu movies. I like making passionate love to a certain beautiful redhead, but then, you already know that." He pointed the fork at me. "Your turn."

"You already know about me. I'm divorced. I'm the oldest of three children. I got married when I was nineteen and thought I'd live happily ever after and it didn't work out that way. I never thought of myself as particularly strong, and, when my husband left, I fell apart."

"But you didn't stay that way."

I sighed. "No. I guess you could say I got fed up and decided to fight back. I'm still fighting."

He stopped eating and leveled a steady gaze on me. "You don't have to fight with me, Phoebe. Though I'm here as backup if you need me."

Some little icy place inside of me melted when he said those words. I didn't know whether to burst into tears or throw my arms around him and kiss him senseless. I settled for eating my dinner and acting unaffected. But my heart pounded with joy, and maybe a little fear. What was I getting into here? I really, really, really didn't want to make another mistake with a man.

A little while later, he took me home. He walked me to the

front door and started to follow me in, but I stopped him. "I think we'd better say good-night now," I said.

He looked puzzled. "Any particular reason why?"

I smiled and stood on tiptoe to kiss his cheek. "Because, I never sleep with a man on a first date."

He was still standing there when I slipped inside, but after a minute or two, I heard him walk away and start his truck. I leaned back against the door and smiled, hugging myself. Tonight had been special. For the things I'd found out about Jeff, and the things I'd found out about myself.

I thought a lot about what Jeff had said about fighting. I'd been passive for so long that standing up for myself was a tremendous rush. But had I gone overboard? How did I know when it was safe to stop the battle and get on with my life?

BY MIDWEEK, THE ENTIRE Clinic building looked like a cut-rate haunted house. Cobwebs dripped from the doorways and pumpkins grinned from every flat surface. Albert stood watch at the entrance to the Family Practice office, nattily dressed in his orange-and-black ball cap and a bow tie that played "Monster Mash" when anyone pressed the button in the middle.

The drug reps ignored Michelle's anti-candy campaign and loaded us down with candy corn, chocolate witches and those sugar-syrup-filled wax lips that taste like crap but look so wonderfully grotesque.

Jerry Armbruster, the Viagra rep, one-upped the competition by bringing in a bagful of candy fangs and what he announced was the ultimate Halloween costume. "What is it?" Michelle asked, holding up what appeared to be a large oval pillow with various straps and buckles dangling from it.

"It's a pregnancy belly." He demonstrated by strapping the contraption over his Brooks Brothers suit.

I don't think words can do justice to the image of a six-foot-tall guy with newscaster-perfect hair and polished wing tips standing there with this huge belly sticking out in front of him. "It looks like some kind of tumor," I said, giggling.

"I suppose you could think of a baby that way." He turned sideways and struck a model's pose. "It's weighted so it puts pressure on the back and kidneys, just like a real pregnancy. They were originally designed to help men develop empathy for their pregnant wives."

"You mean men actually wear these?" Barb gave the belly an experimental poke.

Jerry slipped off the fake fetus and held it up by the straps. "I think it's one of those things that sounds good on paper, but face it girls, the average man wouldn't be caught dead in one of these."

"The guys probably couldn't take it," Michelle said. "I've had three kids and, believe me, pregnancy isn't for wimps."

"The question is, what are you doing with it?" I asked.

"My company makes them," Jerry said. "They're really popular in schools these days. They use them in family-education classes to try to give teenage girls an idea of what a real pregnancy is like. It's supposed to be a great deterrent."

"I can see how it could do the trick." Michelle hefted the belly by the straps. "But what are we supposed to do with it?"

"I thought one of you could wear it to the big Halloween party. Do a pregnant ghoul or something."

"Or the pregnant bride of Frankenstein," Barb added.

"I'll leave it here and let you decide what to do with it." Jerry set it up on the counter. "Now, if I could just have a word with the doctor for a minute?"

I grabbed a handful of chocolate witches to fortify me for the afternoon and headed back to my workroom. Or my dungeon, as Jeff insisted on calling it now that it was draped in cobwebs and black crepe paper.

The intercom buzzed and Barb informed me that I had a call. I hoped it was Frank, telling me that Easy Motors had decided to return my car. Instead, it was Mike Dawson.

"So, how'd you like the story?" he asked.

"It was great. I really appreciate it."

"Has Easy Motors coughed up your car yet?"

I sighed. "No. They haven't said a word about it."

"Not to you, but I've heard plenty. They've threatened to sue me for slander."

"Oh, Mike! I'm so sorry."

He laughed. "Hey, don't worry. I know the law and I haven't done anything wrong. This is actually a good sign. It means we're making them sweat."

"Do you really think they'll break down and give me my car?"

"If we keep at them, I think they will. So what do you think about doing another story? Going back to Easy Motors and giving them some more bad publicity?"

I swallowed. Was all this doing any good, or was I just making a spectacle of myself for nothing? "I don't know, Mike...."

"Come on. Don't give up now. Aren't you tired of riding the bus?"

I took a deep breath. "Okay. If you really think it will help."

"Good girl. I'll meet you there tomorrow morning at eight. That way we'll attract the morning drive-time crowd. You'll see. This is gonna be great."

I WAS AT THE DOOR of the local Quickie Printer's by six that evening. The clerk took one look at my I Bought a Lemon From Easy Motors T-shirt and grinned. "Hey, I read about you in the paper," she said. "Did you get your car yet?"

"Not yet. But I'm working on it. I need your help."

"Sure thing. What do you need?"

Two hours later, I left with two hundred and fifty bumper stickers that read Give Phoebe Her Car. If I was going to be notorious, I figured I might as well go all out.

When Easy Motors opened at eight o'clock the next morning, the Phoebe Frame fan club was there to greet them: me, Mike and Sheila, and Darla, who had dragged Tony along to act as "bodyguard" in case Frank got too forceful with his threats. "It's the least we can do," Darla said when I protested they didn't have to do this. "Besides, I always wanted to be in the papers."

Frank was so stunned by my reappearance that he didn't react right away when I handed him one of my bumper stickers. Sheila snapped a great shot of him holding the sticker, with me grinning next to him.

News Four showed up and filmed me applying a bumper sticker to Tony's truck, and then Channel Two got into the act by interviewing me for a segment on the morning broadcast. The reporter introduced me as a "plucky young woman fighting for her rights." I didn't know which I appreciated more: being called young or a fighter.

Whether because of the time of day or my growing notoriety, an even larger crowd gathered to gawk. I waved and smiled and handed out my bumper stickers to anybody who would take one. A teenage boy put one on his skateboard, and a middle-aged businesswoman plastered one across her briefcase.

Just before nine, a hulking black-and-purple tow truck pulled to the curb and a tall, lanky man unfolded himself from the front seat. "Ben." I welcomed him like an old friend. "This is the wrecker driver who towed my car here in the first place," I told Mike.

Ben scratched his head. "I've felt kind of bad about that ever since. So I stopped by to tell you that if this bunch ever does decide to let your car go, I'll be happy to tow it over to my shop and fix it for free."

When the news went out, a cheer rose up from the crowd. Ben flushed and shuffled his feet. He didn't say "aw, shucks" but he might as well have.

At 9:15, with the crowd showing no signs of dissipating, the receptionist picked her way across the car lot. "Frank sent me out to talk to you," she said.

"Why doesn't he come out himself?" Mike asked.

The receptionist snapped her gum. "He doesn't want to be on TV or in the papers." She glanced around, then spoke to me in a more confidential tone. "To tell you the truth, I think he's a little afraid of you. No woman has ever stood up to him that way before." She giggled. "You've even got me thinking maybe I should ask for a raise."

While it was gratifying to think I had cowed Frank, that wasn't getting me my car back. "What does he want you to say to me?" I asked.

"He says he'll give you your car back now if you'll go away and promise to never come back."

I grinned. "Somebody go tell Ben to fire up the wrecker. I think this means we won."

Before the cheering had died down, Ben had the blue Mustang hooked onto the back of his wrecker and was leading a caravan down Alameda. I rode with Mike and Sheila, who wanted to film the reunion between me and my wheels. While I balked at kissing the dusty hood, I was happy to sit behind the wheel and wave out the window, grinning from ear to ear.

Ben towed the Mustang to his shop and fixed the motor mount and checked out the rest of the car for me. "She's not in that bad a shape," was his final assessment. "You ought to think about getting the radiator flushed before too long."

"I promise I'll bring it in soon," I said. "And this time, I'll pay you for the work."

He shrugged. "I'd say the publicity's worth more than the cost of that motor mount." A grin cracked his gaunt face. "Besides, it was worth it, seeing Frank Adams get his."

I was feeling so good, I decided to take the rest of the morning off. Joan didn't like it, but she stopped short of threatening to fire me. Right now, Jeff and I were the only ones who knew how to work the new transcription system. If she let me go, no one else would ever figure it out.

Darla didn't have to go in to work until later that afternoon, so she followed me back to my house and we celebrated over a lunch of take-out pizza and bargain-bin Lambrusco. "Here's to Phoebe Frame, freedom fighter." Darla raised her glass in a toast.

We clinked glasses and I took a long drink of wine. "I just liberated my car, not an enslaved country."

"You stood up for women everywhere. You showed Sleazy Motors they can't take advantage of someone just because she's female."

"Hmm. I don't feel particularly militant. Just relieved it's all over with. Besides—" I picked a slice of pepperoni off the pizza and popped it into my mouth "—I never could have done it without Mike Dawson and all the publicity he gave me."

"You don't give yourself enough credit."

"You sound like Jeff."

"Oh?" She perked up and leaned toward me. "And what does the boy wonder have to say on the subject?"

I squirmed. "Just what you said, that I don't give myself enough credit. That I have more going for me than I want to admit."

She sat back, a satisfied smirk on her face. "I'd say the man is not only handsome, he's smart. So, are you still playing hard to get?"

"Uh, not exactly." I picked at the cheese on my slice of pizza, stretching it out like a rubber band, then letting it go.

"What do you mean by that?"

"I mean, we've agreed to date."

"Each other?"

"Of course each other." I took a bite and chewed, grateful for a reprieve from talking.

"And?"

I raised my eyebrows at Darla and kept chewing.

"And how's it going?" she prodded.

"It's going all right." I was still confused by my feelings for Jeff. On one hand, I was wildly attracted to him physically, and I enjoyed his company as a friend. On the other hand, I still didn't believe I could ever have anything permanent with him.

I'd rationalized the whole thing by telling myself it was probably better to have at least one "expendable" relationship between one marriage and the next. To make sure I wasn't on the rebound and everything. Isn't that what everybody said? "I'm going to try to have fun with Jeff and not worry about what happens next," I said.

Darla froze, a piece of crust halfway to her mouth. "You, not worry?" She leaned forward and felt my forehead. "Are you okay?"

"I'm fine. More than fine. I'm just great." Not exactly happy with my life, but not unhappy, either. Some days that's the best you can hope for.

The doorbell rang and I jumped. "Expecting someone?" Darla asked.

I shook my head and went to answer it. The only people who ever came to see me, besides Darla, who never rang the bell, were school kids selling something and earnest young men in white shirts and narrow ties who wanted to talk to me about the afterlife. I always told them I had enough troubles handling this life without worrying about the next one.

My visitor today wasn't a school child or an evangelist, though there were times when I thought of him as a particular kind of devil. "Steve, what do you want?"

He pushed past me into the house. "I want the ring. It was my grandmother's and it rightfully belongs to me."

"Do you want me to call the police?" Darla appeared in the doorway to the kitchen, portable phone in hand.

"You can't have a man arrested for being in his own house," Steve said with a sneer.

"It's not your house anymore," Darla snapped.

"Steve, you'd better leave." I tried to sound reasonable, though what I felt bordered on panic. The man said he wanted out of my life—why did he keep showing up like this?

He held out his hand. "The ring."

I put my hands behind my back. "No. The ring belongs to me."

Did I mention that Steve is a master at the condescending look? He wore that look now, an expression that said he was the adult here, trying to deal with a difficult child. "You have the ring now only because I gave it to you. As a symbol of our intention to get married. We're not married anymore, so the ring is meaningless as a symbol."

It sounds so logical, doesn't it? As cold and calculated as the language in our divorce decree itself. "You gave me this ring. You can't just take it back, the way you took back your wedding vows."

He clenched his fists at his sides and anger roughened his voice. "The trouble with you, Phoebe, is that you're so good at playing the victim. This whole fiasco with your car is a perfect example. You didn't bother to tell that reporter that I was the one who bought your other car for you, that I'd given it to you as a gift. And you didn't tell him that when it came time to settle the terms of our divorce, you never said one word about wanting a new car."

I stared at him, assaulted by this twisted logic. "I was in shock. I was too stunned to think about the car."

He shook his head. "There you go again, playing the victim. And the worst part is, you don't even realize you're doing it. Even after the divorce, if you'd bothered to ask my advice on buying a car, I would have told you to have it thoroughly checked out by a mechanic first."

"Why should she bother asking your advice about anything?" Darla took a step toward him. She still had the phone in her hand and I figured any minute now, she'd brain him with it.

I tried to move to intercept her, but my legs felt too wobbly to move. "You'd better go," I said weakly.

"Not until I have the ring."

I twisted the ring on my finger. All of a sudden, it didn't seem to fit so well. Why did I want this particular diamond? I'd thought it was because it represented something important in my life, but now Steve's words had taken even that away. I slipped the ring off my finger. "Phoebe, no!" Darla cried.

I folded my fingers around the diamond and looked at Steve. "I want the money."

His eyes fairly glowed with triumph. "Send the papers to my lawyer and I'll see that it's taken care of."

"No. I want it now." I leaned over and plucked a pen from a shelf by the door. "Write me a check."

"It'll probably be hot," Darla said.

I shook my head. Steve always carried a five-thousand dollar balance in his checking account. That way, he didn't have to pay any check fees.

He hesitated, then pulled his checkbook from his pocket and wrote out a check for four thousand dollars. He handed it to me and I dropped the ring in his hand. "Maybe when you give it to Tami, you'd better tell her it's just a loan, in case things don't work out between you two."

He glared at me, then shoved past me and out the door. The sound of it slamming echoed in the awful stillness he left behind.

Darla came over and slipped her arm around me. "Why did you do it?" she whispered. "Why did you let him win?"

I looked at the empty finger where the ring had been. "He was right. The ring didn't mean anything anymore. I thought it did, but I was wrong."

She patted my shoulder. "Buy yourself something nice with the money. You deserve it."

I nodded. Sure. I could pay off my Visa bill. Buy myself some new shoes.

I rubbed the slight indentation on my finger where the ring had been. I felt strange without it, stranger still without this last tie to Steve. A chapter of my life was officially over. Time to begin another one. With Jeff? Or someone else.

Too bad crystal balls don't work. I'd have given a good chunk of those four thousand presidents to see what the future had planned for me. Call me a coward if you like, but I prefer to call it smart. If you know what's coming, you'll know when to duck.

16

"YOU KNOW A MAN IS SERIOUS when he sends chocolate." Michelle made this announcement a few days later as she delivered a giant heart-shaped box of candy to my workroom. "A bicycle courier just dropped this off for you."

I stared at the gaudy arrangement of satin bows and plastic roses adorning the top of the box. "Who sends a heart when it's almost Halloween?" I asked. "Where would someone find something like that this time of year?"

"Maybe he's been saving it since Valentine's Day." Michelle deposited the box on my desk. "So is it another present from your secret admirer?"

I slipped a card from beneath the ribbon and opened it. "Sweets for my sweetie," I read. No signature.

"He's not exactly original," Michelle said. "Still, I'd be impressed if a guy sent me anything."

I opened the box and studied the assortment of chocolates within. "Do they look stale to you?"

Michelle leaned over and plucked a caramel from its slot. "Mmmmfff...chewy." She swallowed. "Maybe a little stale. But not bad."

"Michelle, Doctor needs you in room two." Joan tip-tapped her way toward us. She frowned at the box of chocolates. "All that candy is very bad for you," she said. "It sets a bad example for the patients."

"I don't think any of the patients will see it back here." I offered her the box. "Would you like a piece? The caramels are especially nice." With any luck, she'd lose a filling and be out of commission for at least a day.

"Put that away and get to work," she ordered, and retreated down the hall, Michelle in her wake.

I replaced the lid on the candy and tried to get back to work. But listening to Patterson relate the amusing story of how a three-year-old swallowed a quarter from the tip tray at a restaurant didn't hold any fascination for me.

I was restless. Edgy. As if I'd suddenly gained ten pounds and none of my clothes would fit right. My life didn't fit right. For twelve years, I'd known exactly what to expect from each day. I'd had the same house, the same job, the same marriage. Now, nothing was the same. I didn't know where I was going or where I wanted to go.

I looked around my workroom. No wonder Jeff called it my dungeon. That's exactly what it felt like. I took off my headphones and tossed them onto the counter. I had to get out of here. At least for a few minutes.

I grabbed up the box of candy and headed up front. "Where are you going?" Joan asked as I passed her.

"You're right. This candy has no place in the office. So I'm going to get rid of it."

I made it onto the elevator just as the doors shut. I had the car to myself, and took advantage of this to study my reflection in the polished steel door. "Phoebe, you need a vacation," I said to the tired-looking woman who stared back at me. "Someplace without ex-husbands, lecherous bosses or sadistic car dealers."

The elevator stopped on the second floor and a pregnant woman got on. I scarcely looked at her, I was so absorbed in my own problems. Besides, it's an unwritten rule that people in elevators don't look at each other or say anything. We all stand in our own little square of silence, facing forward and keeping our mouths shut. And, except in the case of my mysterious groper, our hands to ourselves.

Apparently, this chick didn't know the rules. After a minute, she leaned toward me. "Aren't you Phoebe Frame?"

I turned and stared into an all-too-familiar face. "You!" Just-a-waitress. Tami. The future second Mrs. Steve Frame. We'd never been face-to-face like this before. Of course, I'd thought about meeting her many times. In my fantasies, I either tore out her hair or spat in her face.

But real life isn't like fantasy. I couldn't even think of any cutting remarks. I just stared at her, goggle-eyed. The elevator stopped on the ground floor and the doors started to open, but she leaned over and hit the close button. "We need to talk," she said.

She hit the button for the seventeenth floor and, after a moment, we started back up. "I don't have anything to say to you," I said, and faced forward again.

She took a step back, and put her hands protectively on her belly. "I know you probably hate me, but you shouldn't."

"I shouldn't swear or eat so many sweets, but I haven't been inclined to give them up. Why should I give up hating you?" In fact, I was pretty ticked off that she'd expect me to stand here and listen to her. I leaned over to hit the four. I'd get off and take another elevator back down. But just as my finger touched the button, the car lurched and made a screeching noise.

Everything went silent and still. Tami looked up at the lighted display which showed the number of each floor. Both the three and the four were lit. "Why are we stopped?" she asked.

"I don't know." I started hitting buttons, but nothing happened. "They've been having trouble with the elevators," I mumbled.

"Then we'd better call."

I opened the little door in the control panel and picked up the emergency phone. "Hello, this is Building Services. If you'd like to report a maintenance problem, press one. If you need to order supplies, press two. If you have a question for janitorial services, press three...." I listened with ever-growing irritation, until the recording reached seven. 'If you'd like to leave a message, please record your name and number at the tone.'

"If I had a number, I wouldn't be calling you," I snapped. "We're stuck in the elevator, dammit." I slammed down the receiver and glared at it. Of all the times to get stuck in the elevator. If it had to happen, why couldn't it have been with Jeff? At least he would have made it...interesting.

Tami sank to the floor like a deflated balloon. I scowled at her. "I hope you don't expect me to help you up again."

"I can't stand very long," she whined. "My ankles swell."

I leaned against the opposite wall of the car and pretended not to look at her. But how could I not look at her? If you'd been in a race and lost by inches at the last second, wouldn't you look at the runner who beat you out? Wouldn't you want to know what that runner had that you didn't?

Who was I kidding? I knew what Tami had that I didn't: long blond hair, big boobs and ten fewer years in the birth-date slot on her driver's license. She also had Steve, but as far as that went, she was welcome to him.

"Go ahead and laugh if it makes you feel better," she said.

"Laugh?" I frowned. "Why would I laugh?"

She struggled to sit up straighter. "I know what you're thinking. I used to be thin and pretty, with a glamorous job, and now I'm just fat and pregnant and unemployed. While you stand over there, in your fancy clothes, with your fancy job and...and a box of chocolates. I'll bet you think you have it made." She sounded as if she was going to cry any minute now.

I tried not to let my surprise show on my face. It was true she was looking a little doughy these days, but she had a good excuse. I would have translated "unemployed" to "lady of leisure" but maybe it didn't look that way from her end.

I glanced down at the off-brand suit I'd bought on clearance two years ago. Not what I'd call fancy. And I certainly wouldn't call stuck in a closet all day typing up notes for Patterson a glam position. I did, however, have a box of chocolates. I removed the lid and offered the candy to Tami. "Would you like a piece?"

She looked at me as if she suspected I'd laced them all with poison, but apparently the lure of even stale chocolate was too much for her. She chose a piece and popped it into her mouth.

I watched her chew with cowlike thoroughness and felt a completely unexpected emotion sneak up and poke me in the stomach. Looking at this doughy, fat, stringy-haired person slumped on the floor of the elevator, masticating a stale chocolate, I felt a kind of pity. Not only was she pathetic, she had to put up with Steve. "What did you want to talk to me about?"

"This." She held up one hand.

Any sympathy that had been building for her dried up when my gaze came to rest on her left hand and I saw the ring glinting there. "I could almost forgive you for taking Steve off my hands," I said. "But I'll never forgive you for stealing my ring."

She regarded the jewel. "There's no reason for you to feel that way. It's Steve's grandmother's ring. It ought to stay in the family." She resumed her pouting expression. "Besides, Steven told me you have a new boyfriend who can buy you all the rings you want. A young, good-looking boyfriend."

I blinked. "Steve told you that?"

"He didn't want to, but I made him." She squirmed. "I think it ticked him off that you'd end up with somebody with more hair than he has. He's very sensitive about his hair, you know."

"He's sensitive about a lot of things."

She rolled her eyes. "Tell me about it. I cooked his egg too hard the other morning and he had a hissy."

I nodded. So she was already finding out about the bad side of her glamorous older man. "What did you do?"

She shrugged. "I told him if that's how he felt, he could make his own breakfast."

Now why didn't I ever think of that? I held out the box of chocolates. "Here. Have another piece."

"Thanks."

We were silent for a minute, eating chocolate. "Does Steve still leave his dirty clothes in the middle of the bathroom floor?" I asked after a minute.

"No, I broke him of that one. I told him anything on the floor went in the trash. He didn't believe me until I threw out a brand-new golf shirt."

I winced. "What did he do?"

She shrugged. "Oh, he threw a temper tantrum, but I just put on my headphones and turned up the stereo. I told him if he was going to act like a toddler, I'd treat him like one."

A snort of laughter escaped me. "You should give lessons."

She glanced up at me. "No offense, but you spoiled him. A lot of women do that. But he's coming around. Yesterday he did a load of laundry for the first time. I figure it's a start."

I could see it all so clearly now. I had spoiled Steve—waiting on him, picking up after him. I'd been...like another mother to him. No wonder our love life had suffered.

This revelation hit me hard. I felt like sinking to the floor, too, but managed to stay upright. While I was still trying to absorb this new picture of my marriage, the phone rang.

"Hello?"

"You ladies all right in there?" a man asked.

I glanced at Tami. "We're okay, but one of us is very pregnant. If you don't want her having the baby right here, you'd better get us out pronto."

"We're working as fast as we can. Don't worry."

I hung up the phone and turned to Tami. "They're working on it."

She nodded. "I've noticed people—men especially—are afraid of pregnant women. They're terrified we're going to go into labor and start bleeding on them or something. The other night, we went out to dinner and the service was a little slow. Steve told the waiter I might go into labor any minute and ten minutes later, we had a five-course meal on the table."

I nodded. "So what did you want to say to me about the ring?"

"Just that you did the right thing, giving it up. I appreciate it, and so does Steve, even if he'd never say it."

I wasn't so sure about Steve, but I was ready to let it go. Even though I hated to lose a fight, losing in this case was almost like winning. I'd cut my last ties with my old marriage and my old life. I was starting over. And being four thousand dollars richer for it didn't hurt, either.

The elevator lurched, then we started moving down. "I think it's fixed," I cried.

Tami started to hoist herself up the wall. "Here, let me." I offered my hand. She took it and I helped her stand.

She checked her watch. "That wasn't so bad."

I glanced at her, my old animosity lost somewhere between the third and fourth floors. "No, it wasn't so bad," I said. I pulled the box of candy from under my arm and held it out to her. "Why don't you take this? I really couldn't eat it all."

"Are you sure?"

I nodded. "I'm sure."

She took the heart-shaped box. "I'm already fat, so I guess it doesn't matter if I get a little fatter." She straightened and met my gaze. "I'm glad we had a chance to talk."

"Me, too."

I watched her waddle across the lobby and out the door and thought about all the funny twists and turns life can take. Maybe if I'd told Steve to fry his own eggs, he and I would still be together. Or maybe we'd have beat each other to death with spatulas.

Or maybe, everything had worked out exactly as it was supposed to. Some people believe in that kind of fate. Me, I'm not sure what I believed in, except that maybe my life wasn't so bad after all. Maybe I just had to stretch a little bit, and make it fit.

DARLA WAS MY BEST FRIEND, so that pretty much meant I couldn't kill her. But that didn't mean I wasn't tempted to strangle her when I found out what she'd planned as my costume for the Halloween party. "What am I supposed to be?" I asked, fishing a pair of tiny leather shorts out of the grocery sack she handed me.

"Just put it on. All of it." She pushed me toward the bedroom. "I can't wait to see."

When I unpacked the rest of the stuff in the bedroom, I discovered fishnet stockings, a pair of thigh-high, spike-heeled boots, a leather vest, a studded dog collar and a whip. "Darla, I can't wear this!" I shrieked.

"Yes, you can. Put it on."

Okay, so I'll admit I couldn't wait to see how I'd look in that getup. All that leather...I mean, it's a sexual fantasy waiting to happen.

I put on everything in the bag. The dog collar took a little getting used to, and I felt ten feet tall in those boots. When I finally got up the nerve to look at myself in the mirror, my mouth dropped open. I have to admit, I looked pretty hot. Those tall boots and little shorts made my legs look a mile long, and the vest was just tight enough to make my little bit of cleavage look like a lot.

The door opened and Darla leaned in. "What do you think?"

I swallowed. "I think if I wear this to the party, I'm liable to give Patterson a heart attack, not to mention the wrong idea."

"If he gets out of line, you can always use the whip." She picked up the leather quirt and flicked it at me. "Besides, who cares about Patterson? What do you think Jeff will think?"

The thought of Jeff's potential reaction sent a flush of red from my cleavage up. Darla laughed. "That good, huh?" She handed me the whip. "Then you've got to wear it."

I turned away from the mirror. "Darla, what in the world made you decide I should dress up as a dominatrix?"

"You said you wanted to be a strong woman who wouldn't take shit from anybody and a sexy woman who would have men crawling at her feet." She gestured toward me with both hands. "Tah-dah! Power, command and sex appeal. I'd say it's you."

"I have to work with these people." I tossed the whip onto the bed again. "Joan will have a fit when she sees me."

"Joan probably has a second job running her own dungeon. Come on, this could work to your advantage."

I crossed my arms over my chest. "And just how do you figure that?"

"You said yourself everyone at the office takes you for granted. Well, this will shake them up. They'll realize they don't know everything there is to know about you. They might even be a little afraid of you. And you know what they say—a little bit of fear can translate into a whole lot of power."

"Who says that?" I slipped a finger under the dog collar and scratched.

"Some professors who wrote a book about sexual power. I saw them on *Oprah.*" She tilted her head and studied me. "Remember, lots of eyeliner and mascara and red, red lipstick."

"Can I at least wear a mask? At least then maybe everybody won't recognize me."

"You're no fun." Darla laughed. "But yeah, I brought a mask, just in case you chickened out. But it only covers your eyes." She waggled her eyebrows suggestively. "I made sure to leave your mouth free in case you want to reward some lucky slave with a kiss."

The thought sent a tingle through me. I couldn't be sure if it was nervousness or desire. Part of me was terrified of looking like a fool. The other part couldn't pass up a chance to play the woman in charge for a change. Lord knows, it wasn't a role I ever got to see in real life. I took a deep breath. "Okay. I'll do it. But if I end up without a job, believe me, you—"

"I know, I know. I owe you."

17

WITH MY HAIR TEASED OUT and sprayed with glitter, and a black mask covering my nose and eyes, I held out a slim hope that no one at the party would recognize me. I figured I had the element of surprise on my side. I mean, how many people would expect meek transcriptionist Phoebe Frame to transform herself into Mistress Phoenix?

By the time I got there, the party was already in full swing. A DJ in the main lobby played music that was piped to all the medical suites. Every floor had a buffet with a different theme: Mexican food, Chinese food, barbecue. There were two cash bars plus free rum punch. The top floor had been turned into a haunted house—a mad doctor's operating room with enough real medical equipment to give anybody the creeps.

All my seemingly normal co-workers had transformed themselves into everything from a thirteenth-century knight to a six-foot-tall cockroach that was more horrifying than any run-of-the-mill ghoul. I recognized my friend Beverly from obstetrics, dressed as Dorothy, with a tin man who had to be her husband, Bill. Michelle was a ghoulish nurse, complete with bloodstained uniform and a green fright wig.

Lots of people stared at me as I minced across our office suite in those impossibly tall high heels, and one or two of the men leered, but no one showed any signs of recognition. A thrill rippled through me as I passed people who saw me every day and their faces remained blank. They had no idea that the powerful, sexy woman before them was mild-mannered Phoebe Frame, forgotten transcriptionist. Let me tell you, it was a rush. I understood how superheroes could get addicted to the saving mankind shtick.

I headed for the punch bowl, and a healthy dose of liquid courage. While I ladled rum punch into a paper cup, I searched the crowd for Jeff. He'd refused to tell me what kind of costume he'd chosen. Would he be a vampire? A mummy?

Before I could find Jeff, however, Dr. Patterson found me. Only he didn't realize it was me. He was wearing a Dracula getup, complete with white tie and tails. Owing to his broad shoulders and not inconsiderable bulk, he more closely resembled a penguin on steroids than Vlad the Impaler. "Hellooo," he drawled, and flashed his fangs. "I'm Ken Patterson. Dr. Patterson. I don't believe we've met, Miss...?"

I affected a German accent in case Patterson recognized my regular voice. "Mistress. Mistress Phoenix."

Instead of putting him off, as I'd hoped, my frost-queen act only piqued Patterson's interest. "It's such a pleasure to meet you, Mistress. Uh...may I call you Mistress?"

Oh, what the hell? I thought. When was I going to be in this kind of position again? I gave him an aloof smile. "Only those who please me may call me Mistress."

He sidled a little closer and lowered his voice. "Then what may I do to please you?"

Give me a twenty percent raise? Move to Siberia? I took a step away from him. "I'm hungry," I said petulantly. "Fetch me some shrimp from the buffet."

He didn't even hesitate. "What kind of shrimp do you prefer? We have boiled and fried."

Amazing! "Boiled. And be sure to peel them."

Coattails flapping behind him, he headed for the buffet table in the next room. I took off in the opposite direction. By the time Patterson returned with those shrimp, I planned to be in a distant part of the building.

I was trying to squeeze my way through the crowd to the elevator when somebody grabbed my arm. I whirled and looked down at a pudgy guy wearing red-footed pajamas and horns, who was carrying a pitchfork. His forehead came about level with my chin and his nose stuck out from beneath his black mask like the prow of a ship. "I've been looking for you," the little devil said, grinning up at me.

I shook loose of his hand. "You must have me confused with someone else."

"Oh, no. You're the only woman I want." His grin morphed into a full-blown leer and settled on my cleavage. "I love your costume."

He reached for me again, but I managed to dodge out of his way. "Do not touch Mistress Phoenix," I said in my thickest accent, scowling at him.

He actually giggled! "I love it when you get forceful." He sidled closer. "Maybe later you could spank me?"

I felt nauseated just thinking about it. I took a step back. "Um, I have to go now. I'll be late for the...late for the next door-prize drawing."

I took off, moving as fast as I could through the crowd. It's amazing what having a whip in your hand will do for you. I was almost to the door when I heard someone calling, "Mistress! Oh, Mistress Phoenix!"

I tried to ignore him, but the crowd had me pinned and the next thing I knew, Patterson was at my side, holding a plateful of naked shrimp. "I didn't know if you wanted tartar or red sauce, so I got both," he said.

I stared down at the little pink shrimps. Sure enough, there wasn't a peel on any of them. The thought of eating anything Patterson's hands had been all over turned my stomach further. "Um, I've changed my mind." I leaned over and set the plate on a nearby planter. "I'm not hungry anymore."

The old boy wasn't fazed. He grabbed my hand and pulled me toward the center of the room. "Let's dance."

I jerked my hand away. "Mistress does not dance."

"Then I'll teach you." I watched in horror as he held his hands up over his head and swayed.

"No!" I said, alarmed. "I—I'm thirsty. I want a drink."

"There's punch over here—"

"Not punch. I want a real drink."

He stopped moving. "All right. The bar's downstairs. We'll go get you a drink. Then maybe we can find someplace quiet, where we can get to know each other better."

His fangs glittered as he grinned at me. I shuddered. "No. You get the drink for me."

"But we can go together—"

I glowered at him. "You said you wanted to please me." I stamped my foot. "I want a drink."

His shoulders dropped half an inch, then he rallied. "All right. What sort of drink would you like?"

I searched my brain for the most complicated thing I could think of. "I want a...a martini. Shaken, not stirred. Two olives. In a chilled glass."

He nodded and made an elegant bow. "I shall return."

Fine, but I wouldn't be here waiting for him. As soon as the crowd swallowed him up, I took off toward the stairs. Eleven floors in these heels was going to be a bitch, but it would be worth it to get away from Patterson.

Unfortunately, the doctor wasn't the only one intent on monopolizing my time. The little devil had climbed up onto a desk and was scanning the crowd like a sailor searching for shore. I crouched down, hunting for cover.

A long table had been set up on the side of the room, draped in a white cloth and topped with jack-o'-lanterns and bowls of candy. I duckwalked toward it, then dove under the cloth. I could creep along under here almost to the door, then make a dash for it.

Do you know how difficult it is to creep in spike-heeled boots and tight leather shorts? I dropped to my hands and knees and crawled, fish net digging into my knees. When I saw Darla again...

"Eeeek!" I squealed as a hand grasped my ankle, and whirled to find myself staring into an amused pair of brown eyes.

"Lose something?" Jeff asked.

I crawled out from under the table and stood with my nose buried in a broad, bronzed, naked chest. Well, not altogether naked. Jeff wore a leather vest, leather cuffs and a dog collar that was wider and more heavily studded than my own. And he seemed to be carrying a shield. A whiff of spicy, seductive cologne stirred my senses. I looked up, gaping. "When did you get here?"

He grinned. "I thought I recognized you." His gaze slid appreciatively over my costume. "I have to hand it to you, Phoebe, you're not exactly predictable."

"Shh." I put a finger to my lips and glanced around to see if anyone had heard. But everyone was intent on the door-prize drawing being announced over the loudspeaker. "Call me Mistress Phoenix. I don't want anyone to know who I am."

"All right. Mistress." The word hissed off his tongue like cold water on a skillet, and sent a shiver down my spine.

I stepped back to get a better look at his costume and immediately felt weak at the knees. In addition to the leather vest, cuffs and collar, he wore a short pleated skirt that showed off his fantastic legs and a pair of Roman sandals. "You're a gladiator," I said.

"You get an A." He took my elbow and steered me around

a clot of people. "So whose idea was the dominatrix getup? Yours or Darla's?"

"Darla's. She said I needed to free my inhibitions and act out my fantasies."

"Mmm." His hand skimmed down my back and came to rest on the seat of my leather shorts. "I think I like your fantasies."

I tried to put a little distance between us, but it was tough to do in that crowd. "You are not allowed to touch Mistress Phoenix without permission," I said in my fake German accent.

"And what do I have to do to get permission?" He took his hand off my bottom, but closed the distance between us until a good deep breath would have pressed my breasts into his chest.

I knew I couldn't blame my light-headedness on one cup of watered-down rum punch. I swallowed hard. "I don't think touching is a good idea right now." I glanced at the people milling around us and caught sight of Patterson scanning the crowd. He must have cut in line to get back up here so quickly. He had a martini glass in one hand, and a look of pathetic eagerness on his face. "Quick, I have to hide from Patterson." I grabbed Jeff's arm.

"I know just the place." He pulled me out the door and toward the stairs. We climbed up one flight and emerged in a black-lit hallway.

"Where are we?" I asked.

"Back entry into the Haunted House. Come on."

He pushed open a doorway and I jumped as I came face-to-face with a headless body. "Good evening," said the head, which was sitting on a table beside the body. "Welcome to the Hospital of Horrors."

"Lookin' good, Pete." Jeff gave a thumbs-up to the body.

"Thanks," said a voice from within the body's suit coat. "What are you doing sneaking in the back door?"

"I'm giving Mistress Phoenix here the VIP tour."

We walked on, squeezing past crowds that lined the narrow hallways. In one room, a bug-eyed "surgeon" was sawing off the limbs of a "patient," realistic blood everywhere. Various displays of supposedly real body parts were set out to delight the ghoulish and turn the stomachs of the squeamish. Oversize needles, wicked-looking surgical instruments and miles of bandages and fake blood added extra-authenticity to this house of horrors.

"If people go through this, they'll never want to come to the doctor again," I said as we entered the start of the tour, the waiting room, where a cobweb-covered man with a long gray beard snoozed in the corner. A sign identified him as the true horror of the doctor's office—the forgotten patient.

"Nah, people love this stuff," Jeff said, pushing open a door that led into the corridor. "Money from the entry fees goes to the Cancer Society. It's one of their biggest fund-raisers of the year."

"And how do you know so much about it?" I asked.

"I helped set up the computer-animated special effects."

"You know how to do that stuff?" I was impressed.

He gave me a wicked grin. "I have a lot of special talents you don't know about." He leaned forward, as if to kiss me, when a familiar voice sounded in the room we'd just left. "Has anyone here seen a tall dominatrix?"

"It's Patterson!" I wailed.

"Come on. In here." Jeff took my hand and pulled me down the hall, into a darkened exam room, and shut the door behind us.

The noise of the party receded into the background and, in the darkness, our breathing sounded loud and a bit labored.

Jeff slid his hand down my spine and my heart pounded wildly. "I said, no touching."

"How about kissing?" His lips brushed the back of my neck, warming every nerve ending. He pulled me close, his erection pressed into my back. "It's been a long week," he whispered into my ear. "I've missed you."

My only answer was a low groan. I turned in his arms and kissed him full on the mouth. What can I say? It was probably the only chance I'll ever have to put my hand up some guy's skirt.

Though we were both plenty turned on, we didn't feel the need to rush. We were past the first deprived-and-depraved stage and into the getting-to-know-you phase of lovemaking. So we indulged in long, slow, wet kisses and the kind of extended petting you do when you know you're going to end up having intense, mind-blowing sex. We peeled back layers of clothing, but didn't undress all the way, using the costumes to help set the scene.

The exam table wasn't a bed, but it was flat and cushioned, so it wasn't a bad substitute. And the stirrups did provide a useful place for me to rest my feet, after all.

I may have gotten a little carried away. I can't say for certain I didn't moan a little loudly. Or maybe I even screamed. But honestly, who could have heard me over the din of that party?

I would have been content to lie there all night in Jeff's arms, but the setting itself wasn't exactly conducive to relaxation. "We'd better go before someone comes in and finds us," Jeff said. He sat up and reached for his vest.

Reluctantly, I dressed also. At the last minute, I remembered to put my mask back on. "Maybe it would be better if we didn't leave together," I said.

He nodded. "All right. I'll meet you in the parking lot in fifteen minutes."

I nodded. He left first and, five minutes later, I followed. All I had to do was make it through the crowd and down to the lobby without being recognized, and I'd be home free.

By this time of night, only the serious party-goers remained. The buffets looked as if a horde of locusts had descended on them, the carved pumpkins had burned down to blackened husks and the punch contained significantly more rum than fruit juice. The DJ was fielding requests for "I Put a Spell on You" and "Werewolves of London" and those couples who hadn't sneaked off to various nooks and crannies weren't so much dancing as engaged in rhythmic groping.

I was almost to the elevator when a leering Dracula materialized at my side. "Mistress. I was so afraid you'd left without me."

I ground my teeth together and resumed my Marlena Dietrich impression. "Doctor, where is my martini?" I demanded.

He blinked. "When I couldn't find you, I threw it away."

"You could not find me? You did not look hard enough."

He actually flinched. Oh, my. This was too much fun. "Do you think I am going to make things easy for you?" I snapped. "As mistress, my job is to make things very difficult. You must prove you are man enough for me."

"Yes, Mistress. Certainly. I'll bring you another drink." He turned to go, and collided with a short, big-nosed devil.

I groaned. Why did I attract such freaks?

"Ph-Phoebe!" the little devil slurred drunkenly. "Your costume is f-f-fabulous!" He leaned toward me, a besotted smile across his face. "You're the most beautiful woman in the room."

"Phoebe?" Dr. Patterson's face paled beneath his Dracula greasepaint. His eyebrows came together, then sprang apart. "Phoebe Frame?"

"Who are you?" I demanded of the drunken devil.

"Eddie." He smiled dreamily. "Eddie Parker."

"Do I know you?" It was hard to tell when you're talking to a man who probably doesn't ordinarily run around in red pajamas.

"I work upstairs, in accounting. I see you in the elevator a lot." He leaned closer and the alcohol on his breath made my eyes water. "Did you like the flowers I sent? And the candy?"

The hair on the back of my neck rose up. My secret admirer. "You're the groper!" I said, and moved toward him.

He jumped back, and trod on Patterson's toe. The doctor had recovered from the shock of finding me out, and glowered at me. "You did this on purpose," he said. "You set out to make a fool of me."

"I didn't set out to do anything but come to a costume party," I said. "Anything else that happened, you did all by yourself."

"This won't be the last you hear of this."

"Don't threaten me." I tried to sound brave, and hoped he wouldn't notice the shaking in my voice.

"That's exactly what I'm doing." His voice was a menacing growl. I leaned away from him, shaking in my boots. "You'll be sorry you ever crossed me." He gave me a cutting look, then swept his cape around himself and stalked away, looking more like Dracula than he had all evening.

I stared after him, telling myself I wasn't going to make things any better by throwing up in public, though fear had whipped my insides into pudding. Would Patterson really do something to harm me? Something physical? Or would he think of something worse?

"Mistress, now that we're alone we can talk."

I turned to Eddie, who was still grinning at me. "Get lost!" I snapped, and raised my whip.

He tripped over his tail in his hurry to get away, and ended up carrying it in one hand and the pitchfork in the other. I made it to the parking lot uninterrupted, and found Jeff leaning on my car. "I thought I was going to have to go back in after you."

"I ran into Patterson again."

"Oh?" Jeff took my keys and unlocked my door. "Did he give you any trouble?"

"He knows who I am now. And he wasn't happy about it."

"How did he find out?"

"There's this little guy who gropes me in the elevators sometimes. Apparently, he has some kind of crush on me and he recognized me and said my name when Patterson was within earshot."

"He gropes you in elevators?" Jeff clenched his fists, as if he was ready to pound the man in question.

"Some guys get off on that, you know?" I waved the topic aside. "Anyway, Patterson is really ticked now. I think he might fire me."

"Can he do that? Fire you for coming to a costume party?"

"He'll say it's something else. That I wasn't getting my work done. Or that I have a bad attitude. Which is true." I slumped in the seat. "What am I going to do? I need this job."

"You may need a job, but it doesn't necessarily have to be this one."

"Easy for you to say. You own your own company."

"You could come work for me."

I looked up at him, trying to judge whether or not he was serious. "Right. Doing what? I don't know anything about computers."

"You know about the transcription program. You could train people in the offices where I install it."

"No, thanks. It's bad enough that we've worked together here. The last thing I'd want is for you to be my boss."

"You'd be in for all kinds of extra benefits." He caressed my shoulder.

"I could sue you for sexual harassment."

"Promise?"

He reached for me, but I pushed him away. "I think I've had enough excitement for one night. I just want to go home and think about this."

"You mean brood."

"Don't knock it. It's one of the few things I'm good at."

He leaned over and kissed me on the cheek, a sweet, comforting gesture. "You're good at a lot more than that, Phoebe. Don't you forget it."

He opened the car door and slid out. "I'll call you."

I nodded and started the engine. "Good night, Jeff. And thanks."

"Thanks for what?"

"Mainly for not being a jerk-off, like every other man I know."

He stepped back from the car. "I think I'll take that as a compliment."

I laughed and drove away. When I looked back, he was still standing there in the parking lot, a tall man in a short skirt who, little by little, was turning my life upside down.

18

I DIDN'T SLEEP VERY WELL that night, between imagining all the ways Patterson would find to make my life hell and wondering what I was going to do about Jeff. I mean, I liked the guy a lot. And the sex was great. But there ought to be something more going for a relationship than great sex, don't you think?

Me, I can scarcely think at all before my first cup of coffee. I was waiting for it to brew when someone knocked on the back door. I didn't have to guess who it was. Darla always comes to the back door, and I knew she'd be anxious to hear how her costume creation had gone over.

"Morning, Darla," I said when I opened the door. It was much too early yet to tell if it was good or not.

"Guess what?"

I blinked at her. She was wearing cat's-eye sunglasses, a pink polka-dot sundress and a bubble-flip hairdo right out of the pages of *Seventeen* magazine—circa nineteen sixty-seven. "You've been impregnated by an alien," I said.

She lowered the sunglasses and stared at me over them. "No. Have you?"

A gladiator, maybe, but not an alien. I shuffled back to the coffeemaker and stared at the black gold slowly dripping into the carafe. "What have you done to your hair?"

She patted the solid curve of the flip. "It's leftover from my costume. But it's part of what I rushed over here to tell you about."

I poured a cup of coffee for me, then filled a second mug for

Darla. "Tell. Just don't expect much response until the coffee kicks in."

She accepted the coffee and followed me to the table. "Tony and I have decided on a theme for our wedding. We got the idea from our costumes last night."

I looked at her hair again. "You went as Barbie and Ken?"

She laughed, a sound that was entirely too cheerful to be made before noon. "No, silly! We went as Elvis and Priscilla. We're going to have an Elvis wedding! Isn't that fantastic?"

Fantastic was not the word I'd have chosen. Different, maybe. Innovative. Well, how about downright weird? "An Elvis wedding." I furrowed my forehead trying to imagine Tony as Elvis. "Young, sexy Elvis, or old, fat Elvis?"

"Young and sexy, of course."

"But...Tony doesn't have any hair. I'm pretty sure Elvis had hair."

She waved aside this minor discrepancy. "Tony's going to be a bald Elvis. He can do the sideburns, you know. And you should see him in his black shirt and gold chains."

"What exactly is involved in an Elvis wedding?"

"That's what I need your help with. We have to decide on all the details. The dress is easy. I'm going to wear a white lace minidress and go-go boots. Tony's going to grow his sideburns and wear black. But you have to help with the rest."

The last thing I felt like doing was planning a wedding. But maybe this is what I needed to get my mind off my own problems. And really, how hard could this be? "You could rent a pink Cadillac for the ride to the reception," I said.

"That's a great idea. See, I knew I could count on you. Do you have any paper? We should write this stuff down."

Somewhat revived by the coffee, I went in search of a notebook. I found one in the living-room desk and was on my way back to the kitchen when the doorbell rang. I hesitated. It probably wasn't anyone I wanted to talk to, but still...

I stood on tiptoe and peered through the peephole. A big brown eye stared back at me. My lips instantly produced a smile, though I'd have sworn I didn't have one left in me.

I opened the door and grinned like an idiot at the man standing there. "Jeff, you're out and about early."

He was wearing jeans and a polo shirt, but in my mind's eye, he was still in his gladiator's costume. Parts of me woke up just thinking about it.

"I stopped by to see if you were okay."

The words made me feel all sappy and squishy inside.

"Aww, isn't that sweet?"

I might have been thinking something along those lines, but it was Darla who actually spoke. She strolled into the living room, beaming at us both. "Why wouldn't Phoebe be okay?"

Her smile slipped away as she glanced from me to Jeff and back again. "Did something happen at the party last night?" she asked. "Or afterward?"

Jeff stepped into the room and shut the door behind him. "Hello, Darla. Do you have any more of that coffee?"

We all trooped into the kitchen and emptied the coffeepot, then started another one brewing. Darla fussed with sugar and creamer, then sat at the table and fidgeted until she looked like Barbie with a bad case of PMS. "Are you going to tell me what happened last night, or not?" she demanded at last.

Jeff glanced at me. I nodded. What the hell?

"Dr. Patterson really went for that dominatrix getup you fixed up for Phoebe," he said.

She rested her chin on her hand and studied him. "And what did you think of it?"

The smile that spread over his lips was positively lethal. I had to bite my lip to hold back a moan. "I liked it," he said, in a voice that suggested my costume ranked just behind breathing on his top-ten list of favorite things.

Darla stuck her tongue out at me. "What did I tell you?"

"The problem is, Patterson liked the costume entirely too much," I said. "He didn't realize it was me in it."

"If he didn't know it was you, what's the problem?"

I squirmed. "You might say I got a little too into the role."

"What—did you hit him with your whip or something?"

"Not that into it! No, I just ordered him around. Talked down to him. He ate it up."

"Sounds like fun to me. Giving the bastard a little of his own medicine."

"Trouble is, Patterson found out it was Phoebe, after all," Jeff said. "Now he's flamed."

"Ooooh." Darla's lips formed a perfect O. "What did he do?"

"Nothing, yet," I said. "But I have a feeling Monday is not going to be a good day at the office."

Darla leaned over and patted my hand. "Don't worry. I'm sure you can find another job."

"Yeah, I know. But it's such a hassle. I mean, when is it going to end? My life has been one big hassle ever since—" I stopped and glanced at Jeff.

"Ever since your divorce? Hey, I'm a big boy. You don't have to protect my tender feelings." He sipped coffee, looking thoughtful. "I think life is mostly hassles. It makes the good times stand out that much more."

Maybe that's why the time I spent with Jeff had come to mean so much to me, though I wasn't ready to admit that yet.

"I should come back some other time." Darla slid out of her chair and started toward the door.

"Don't go." I felt like a louse. Here she'd come to me with

wonderful news and I'd been about as enthusiastic as a slug. "I want to help you with the wedding."

"Wedding?" Jeff, who was standing now, also, looked at Darla. "Who's getting married?"

"I am," she said.

"Congratulations."

She grinned. "Thanks. Just before you came in, I was telling Phoebe that Tony and I have decided on an Elvis wedding."

"An Elvis wedding?" Somehow, he managed to keep a straight face.

"Yes. With Elvis music and decorations and stuff. Phoebe said we should get a pink Cadillac to take us to the reception."

"Are you going to serve fried-peanut-butter-and-banana sandwiches?"

"Hey, great idea! And RC Cola and MoonPies."

"You'll have lots of music to choose from. 'Love Me Tender,' 'Teddy Bear,' 'Only You'..."

"I have to write this stuff down." She grabbed up the pad of paper I'd brought in from the living room and scribbled madly. "This is all great. Wait till I tell Tony." She ripped off the sheet of paper and stuffed it into her purse. "I really do have to go now. I have a ten-thirty perm at the shop." She gave me a quick hug, then rushed out the door. "Blue Suede Shoes" blasted from her car as she roared away.

"You don't think she'll have the bridesmaids dress like the inmates in 'Jailhouse Rock,' do you?" Jeff asked.

"I don't think she'll go quite that far." I leaned back against the kitchen counter and studied him. "What now?"

"What do you mean, what now?"

"I'm not sure how to take you, Jeff. I mean, what do we really have going on here besides a series of quickies at the office?"

"I'd like to think that we're friends."

I folded my arms across my chest. "Friends?"

"Very good friends." He leaned against the counter beside me.

"Is that all?"

"I suppose that's up to you. You're the one who's always protesting we won't work as a couple."

"I guess I can't figure out if you're leading me on, or if it's the other way around," I said.

"Are you asking me if my intentions are serious?"

The old-fashioned language made me blush. Or maybe it was just knowing that I was putting him on the spot that embarrassed me. "I guess that's what I'm asking."

He looked down at the toes of his shoes and didn't say anything for a long moment. The coffeepot gurgled, a dog down the street started barking and I wished fiercely I could take back the question. It's true that sometimes ignorance is bliss.

At last, he raised his head and his eyes met mine. "I guess my answer is that my intentions are as serious as you want them to be."

What kind of answer is that? Apparently, the only answer I was going to get, since he didn't elaborate. Instead, he took my hand in his and rubbed the knuckle of the third finger. "Why aren't you wearing the ring?"

I'd never thought of myself as having particularly dainty hands, but they looked small and delicate against his broad palm. "I sold it to Steve for four thousand dollars."

"I thought you said it meant more to you than money."

I took my hand away and busied myself rinsing coffee cups. "I guess I lied."

"What did he say to get you to let him have it?"

"Oh, no." I shook my head. "I'm not going to tell you all my secrets."

"I'd settle for even one." He moved away, toward the door to the living room. "Just because I've got a Y chromosome, doesn't mean I'm the enemy. If you're going to be angry with men, be angry with the ones who deserve it."

Before I could answer, he left the room. I was still drying my hands when I heard the front door slam, and the sound of his truck starting.

I stood there with the dish towel in my hand and thought about giving in to a good cry. But I was sick of crying. Sick of whining and moaning about what I didn't have. I knew a better way to fight these blues.

I went into the bathroom and put on some makeup and combed my hair, then picked up my purse and headed out the door. You've heard the saying, haven't you: when the going gets tough, the tough go shopping. Well I had four thousand dollars to spend.

MONDAY MORNING I walked into work wearing a Narciso Rodriguez suit and Manolo Blahnik sandals. If I was about to be unemployed, I was determined to go out in style. Besides, there's nothing like a new outfit to give a woman a boost of much-needed confidence.

On the elevator ride up, I felt someone staring at me. With a feeling of dread, I turned and scowled at Eddie. He grinned. "You're really looking hot this morning, Phoebe." He sidled up to me and lowered his voice. "Would you have my love child?"

"Eddie, I know where a lot of sharp scalpels are kept," I said. "Don't make me use one."

He blanched and sidestepped to the other end of the car. When we reached my floor, I took a deep breath and held my head up as I strode into the office. "Oooh, don't you look snazzy," Michelle said as I passed her.

The office looked as though the building itself was suffering from a bad hangover. Crepe paper drooped from the ceiling and burnt-out jack-o'-lanterns squatted in various stages of decay. Albert leaned drunkenly on his stand, his bow tie half-off, his hat missing altogether. Joan stood in the middle of the office, hands on her hips, frowning at the general chaos. "Take away these pumpkins at once," she ordered, though it was unclear to whom she was speaking. "And get rid of that crepe paper."

I retreated to my office and began undecorating. I rolled cobwebs into balls and wondered if I'd even be around to string Christmas lights.

I tried to get some work done, but aside from a few notes from hospital rounds, there wasn't much to keep me occupied. I debated confronting Patterson myself, and putting an end to this torturous waiting.

At ten o'clock, Joan paged me and told me the doctor wanted to see me. I walked down the hall to his office like a fifth grader on her way to the principal's office. When I opened the door, he looked up from his desk. "Ah, Phoebe. Or do you prefer Mistress Phoenix?"

"The dominatrix getup was just a costume." I forced myself to move closer to the desk. I didn't want him to know how nervous I was. "It was just a gag."

"Too bad." He returned his attention to the patient chart in front of him. I doubted he was really reading it. He was playing a game, making me wait.

"You wanted to see me?" I prompted.

He glanced up at me, then closed the chart and stood. "Yes, I did, Phoebe. I think it's time you and I laid our cards on the table."

I frowned. I didn't like the sound of that. As far as I knew, he held all the cards.

He moved around to the front of the desk and stood with his hands behind his back. "I know the truth, Phoebe, though you've done your best to play hard to get. But Saturday night showed me your true colors."

Things weren't getting any clearer. "I told you the dominatrix outfit was just a costume," I said. "I was just playing around."

He smiled, a thin, superior smile. "You can pretend all you like, but I know the truth."

I crossed my arms over my chest and shifted my weight to one side. "And what is the truth?"

"I know you're hot for me, Phoebe. I've known it from the first day you turned me down. It's high time we quit playing around. I'm ready to accept you as my mistress. Believe me, it's a move you won't regret."

I gaped at him. If he'd just announced he was giving me a raise, I couldn't have been more stunned. My first thought was to tell him to take a flying leap, but some instinct for self-preservation, not to mention job preservation, made me choose my words more carefully. "I'm not interested," I said, and clamped my lips shut.

He tut-tutted and shook his head. "I'm disappointed in you, Phoebe. I had really hoped you would show more intelligence."

"Selling myself to the highest bidder doesn't strike me as all that smart," I said.

He looked sorrowful. "Then I'm afraid you leave me no choice but to let you go."

"You're firing me?"

"It would be impossible for us to work together any longer, considering the circumstances."

"You can't fire me. I'll sue."

He walked back around the desk and picked up the folder he'd been perusing when I came in. "This is your personnel file," he said. He pulled out a sheet of paper and scanned it, lips pursed. "Let's see. It says here that you've taken off three days in the last six months without providing either advance notice or sufficient medical excuse. You've also been late six days and left early another seven days. Yet, at the same time, you've logged almost forty hours in overtime."

"I had to work overtime to keep up with the extra work you gave me," I protested.

He leaned toward me, hands knuckled on the desk. "It has also come to my attention that you are having an affair with one of our contractors, in direct violation of company policy."

I blanched. "There isn't a company policy like that."

"If you had attended the last staff meeting, you would know that there is." He closed the folder. "In light of all this, would you like to consider my offer again?"

Only my ladylike upbringing and a lifelong indoctrination against spreading germs kept me from spitting in his face. I squared my shoulders and spoke with all the dignity I could muster. "You don't have to fire me. I'm resigning. I'll find a better job. One that makes use of my real talent." Whatever the hell that turned out to be.

19

I'D LIKE TO BE ABLE TO SAY that I made a dramatic exit from the office, but the truth was, Michelle was busy trying to draw blood from an uncooperative three-year-old, Joan was helping to hold the child down and Barb was trying to calm the hysterical mother. So I gathered my things and left without anyone even noticing I was going.

As I rode the elevator down to the lobby, I wondered how long it would be before anyone realized I'd left. Even then, would they miss me? Within a few days, some other transcriptionist would be installed in my workroom, and, pretty soon, everyone would forget all about me. Even Eddie would find another crush before too long. Maybe even someone who would return his affections.

There's nothing like being fired to put you in that kind of morbid mood. It didn't help matters any when I reached my car and found a flyer stuffed under the windshield wiper. I pulled it out, expecting one of those cheesy video-store come-ons, but instead, I read: Are you looking for a new career? Houston Technical Institute can train you for an exciting new career in medical technology, medical transcription, nursing, X-ray technology and many other rewarding positions in the medical field. Call 555-8888 to learn more.

"No thanks." I crumpled the paper into a ball and tossed it into the back seat. I'd had one "exciting" career in the medical profession and hadn't found it to be particularly rewarding. I didn't want another job that had anything to do with doctors or hospitals. But since I'd managed to screw myself out of unemployment benefits by quitting before Patterson could fire me, I had to find some kind of job, quick.

On the way home, I stopped at the grocery store and bought a box of double-fudge brownie mix and a paper. While the brownies baked, I could check the want ads for my next "exciting" new career. I would have liked to take a few days to mope, but my bank-account balance told me I didn't have that luxury.

I hung my new suit in the closet and consoled myself with the fact that I had at least one killer outfit to wear to interviews, then pulled on old sweats and mixed up the brownies. One of the nice things about being single is that if you feel like overdosing on chocolate for supper, there's no one around to tell you, you can't.

The *Houston Banner* had one of the biggest want-ads sections in the country, and you'd think those pages would be filled with great, high-paying jobs for a woman with clerical skills. Not.

Unless you call assistant manager at a fast-food joint or night clerk at the local video store the hot new careers of the future. Along with day-care workers and dump-truck drivers, these seemed to be the biggest job markets out there.

Team player needed for fast-paced business with growth opportunities. If you're up to any challenge, call us. Translation: want to be overworked and underpaid and work with a bunch of misfits just like you?

Dot-com start-up seeks creative, high-energy individuals to get in on the ground floor of this exciting opportunity. Work eighty hours a week for worthless stock options.

Exciting position in restaurant franchising. Supervise your own team and reap the rewards. Manage a burger place and have fun coercing a dozen hormonal teenagers into showing up for work on a regular basis. All the fried food you can eat.

I pulled the brownies out of the oven and poured a glass of milk. Say what you want, but warm brownies and cold milk are better than any tranquilizer. I returned to my search of the paper. Hmm, an amusement park was looking for an alligator wrestler. Did fending off Patterson's advances qualify as experience?

Disgusted, I flipped the paper over and was surprised to see my own face staring back at me. Woman Wins Fight with Car Lot read the caption. I scanned the brief story that told of my fight with Easy Motors and their agreement to release my car. "Phoebe Frame's story shows what one person standing up for her rights can accomplish."

I smiled. I had done something good, hadn't I? Too bad I couldn't turn that into some kind of gainful employment. I grabbed the scissors and cut out the photo and article. Maybe I'd make copies and include it with my résumé. Some businesses might get a kick out of having a local celebrity on staff.

I could dream, couldn't I?

I was working my way through my third brownie when the phone rang. "I was calling to see how you're doing," Jeff said.

I set aside the brownie and licked my fingers. "You know, this is becoming a habit with you."

"Does it bother you?"

I smiled. "I think I like it."

"When I stopped by the office this afternoon, Barb told me Patterson had fired you."

"I wasn't fired. I quit."

"Only because he didn't give you any choice."

I leaned back against the counter. "Oh, he gave me a choice. I could have chosen to become his mistress."

"The bastard!"

What did it mean that Jeff's anger on my behalf pleased me

so much? "He has this delusion that I'm secretly in love with him."

"Give me five minutes alone with him and I'll give him delusions."

I chuckled. "I love it when you play the tough guy."

"You seem to be taking this pretty well."

"Yeah, I guess I am, at that." To tell the truth, I felt as if I'd just taken off a too-tight girdle. "I guess that job wasn't a good fit for me anymore," I said. "It was time I left. This is going to force me to do something else with my life instead of spending it stuck in a closet in the back of a building."

"So what are you going to do?"

"I guess tomorrow I'll start sending out résumés. Maybe do some temp work until I find something permanent."

"No, I mean, what are you going to do about Patterson?"

I frowned. "I don't even want to think about that man. Besides, what can I do?"

"I heard talk around the office. Apparently, you aren't the first woman he's done this to."

I sneaked another bite of brownie. "No, there must be half a dozen of us."

"Then somebody ought to stop him."

"And you think I should be that somebody?"

"Why not? You don't strike me as a coward."

Where did he get these vaulted opinions of me? "Maybe not. But I'm not into fighting losing battles, either."

"There must be something you can do. Maybe if all of you got together—"

"Jeff, it's awfully sweet of you to be so indignant on my behalf, but, really, it's best if I just forget this and get on with my life. Patterson is holding all the cards. I don't have any proof of what he's done. And, besides, he doesn't care what us lowly peons think. He only cares about what his colleagues think. That's why this speech is so important to him. The men and women he's speaking before are the ones who count to him."

"Yeah, men like that make me sick."

I pictured Patterson standing up on the podium at the annual Texas Medical Association conference, preening in the spotlight. Those other doctors would listen to him and think what a great physician he was, and never know that he was also a lousy human being.

Sometimes brilliant ideas come from the strangest places. Like in an idle daydream while chewing a brownie. "Jeff, I just had an idea about how I might make Patterson pay for all the harm he's done."

"Now you're talking. What's the plan?"

I shook my head. "I have to see if I can pull it together first."

"Let me help."

"No. I mean, that's really sweet, but I need to handle this myself."

"You don't trust me."

"It's not that." A thrill of anticipation ran through me. "I guess you could say it's a matter of pride."

"I don't understand you. First, you don't like my suggestion to do something, now you can't wait to go after the guy."

"Maybe you inspired me." I dug the phone book out of the drawer and began flipping through it. "I have to go now, Jeff. I have some calls to make."

"Goodbye, Phoebe. Have I told you lately that you're one of the most intriguing women I've ever met?"

"Is intriguing the same thing as confusing?"

"In your case, it just might be."

I laughed. "Bye, Jeff."

"Goodnight, Phoebe. And good luck."

I hung up the phone and dug out a pad of paper. I had lots

to do if I was going to pull this off. And I'd need more than a little luck to make it happen.

I TOOK ADVANTAGE of my first full day as an unemployed person by sleeping late. After more brownies for breakfast, I polished up my résumé and headed to the copy place.

"Hey, how's it going?" The clerk greeted me like her long-lost cousin.

"Uh, hi." I faked a big smile, but she must have clued in to my confusion.

"I helped you print those bumper stickers, remember?" She pointed to a bulletin board beside the cash register. There, above one of my Give Phoebe Her Car bumper stickers was the article from the paper. "You're my most famous customer," she said. "What can I do for you today?"

"I need to make copies of my résumé."

"Thinking of using your notoriety as a springboard to a new career?"

I blinked. "Uh, yeah."

"Springboard. It's one of those 'business' words they teach us to use in this brochure." She pulled a folder out from under the counter and handed it to me.

"Twenty-three ways to energize your résumé." I glanced down the list of suggestions. Buzzwords like *springboard, actualize* and *optimize* jumped out at me. "Um, maybe I should read this before I send anything out."

"Let's see what you got here." The clerk held out her hand and I reluctantly handed over my masterpiece.

She read through it silently, nodding her head and making encouraging noises in her throat. "Skilled at juggling multiple tasks. What does that mean?"

"I can eat lunch and type at the same time."

"That's good. How about great organizational abilities?"

I flushed. "I was the fastest alphabetizer in secretarial school."

She grinned and returned the résumé to me. "Phoebe, you don't need that brochure. You could have written it."

She made twenty copies for me, and even supplied nice mailing envelopes. "Remember, presentation is very important," she said solemnly. "Do you need anything else? Thank-you cards? Business cards? Stationery?"

"Do you do transparencies? You know, for overhead projectors?"

"Sure. We can do photos, graphs, charts...."

I leaned forward and lowered my voice. "I'm planning a little, um, thank-you gift for my former boss," I said. "And I need your help. But it has to be top secret."

The clerk's expression reminded me of a spaniel I once had. You might be on your way to the vet to have him neutered, but tell him he would get to ride in the car and his ears perked up and he'd knock you over on his way to the garage. "I can do it."

"Good. Here's what I have in mind...."

MY NEXT STOP WAS THE OFFICE. Joan Lee met me at the front desk. "You aren't supposed to be here," she said. "Former employees aren't allowed access to the office."

"I just need to pick up a few things I left behind." I tried to move past her, but she put out her arm to block me. For a little woman, she was surprisingly strong.

"Come on, Joan, it's not like I'm going to sabotage the EKG machine or something."

"If you want anything, you can tell one of us and we'll get it for you."

I leaned against the counter. "Fine. I just need the number for Jerry Armbruster."

"The pharmaceutical rep?" Barb flipped through her Rolodex.

Joan frowned. "Why do you need his number?"

None of your business, Joan. I pasted on a fake smile. "I heard his company was looking to hire people."

"You think you could be a drug pusher?" Barb handed me a business card.

"Why not? I've watched plenty of them at work." I patted my hair. "Might have to upgrade my wardrobe and hairstyle. Get a better car."

Apparently convinced I wasn't going to sneak in and make off with a gross of tongue depressors, Joan went back to her office. When she was gone, Barb leaned toward me. "How are you doing?" she asked.

I shrugged. "Okay. Doing the whole job-hunting thing. Listen, I need a few more numbers from you."

"Sure." She reached for her card file.

"Do you have current phone numbers for Kathleen and Gail?"

Her eyes grew wide. "Joan might have them. I don't."

I made a face. "I doubt if Dragon Lady will let me have them without an interrogation."

Barb bit her lip. "Well...I'm not supposed to do this, but they're both still patients here."

"Then the numbers would be in their patient records."

She nodded and tapped her keyboard. After a few minutes, she scratched two numbers on a sticky note and slid it across the counter to me.

"Thanks." I tucked the note in my purse. "Have they hired a new transcriptionist yet?"

"No. They've decided to use a service. They even have Jeff taking out the equipment." She grinned. "Want me to let him know you're here?"

"No, that's okay."

"Barbara, don't you have work to do?" Joan stood in the doorway of her office, scowling at us.

"I'd better go," I said. "Thanks."

I was waiting for the elevator when Jeff emerged from the clinic. "Why didn't you tell me you were here?" he asked.

"I didn't want to disturb you." I glanced back toward the office. "No sense getting you on Joan's bad side, too."

"Does Joan have a good side?" He touched my arm. "How's it going?"

"Good. I got twenty copies of my résumé printed up this morning and I have a few leads for jobs."

"What about your, um, project?"

"That's going good, too."

"Still won't tell me what's going on?"

I smiled. "That depends. Can you still hack into Patterson's computer?"

"Maybe." He put his arm around me and walked me farther down the hall. "You're not thinking of doing anything illegal, are you? Like corrupting files?"

"I just want to know if you can go in and add some files. Nothing obscene or untrue," I hastened to add.

"I could probably do that, if I agreed it wasn't illegal. I'd have to come back after hours."

"Can you do it this week? Before Patterson's talk on Saturday?"

"How about Friday night?"

"That would be perfect."

He glanced back toward the office. Joan was watching us, lips pursed in displeasure. "Why don't I pick you up Friday about seven and we'll see what we can do?"

"Great. And thanks."

He grinned. "That's all I get? Thanks?"

I winked at him. "Let's see what kind of job you do, then we'll discuss payment."

I sashayed back to the elevator, with an exaggerated sway of my hips. I could hear Jeff's laughter all the way down the hall. I felt like laughing myself. So many bad things had happened; my new ability to laugh at them was probably the biggest victory of all.

20

HAVING MAXED OUT my credit card at the Quickie Printer's, I set about job hunting in earnest. Wearing my new designer duds and armed with my guaranteed-to-impress portfolio complete with newspaper clippings, I staged a frontal assault on an assortment of law offices, real-estate firms and computer consortiums. My plan was to land some sort of clerical position with enough pay and benefits to keep me in Diet Coke and coffee. I'd consider almost any field, as long as it didn't have anything to do with medicine.

I started the day with high hopes. After all, I looked great, I felt great and I did great work. What employer wouldn't be happy to have me?

Apparently, the Rose Law Firm was less than impressed. "We're looking for someone with legal experience," Anson Rose told me as he frowned at my résumé.

I scooted forward on the upholstered chair across from his desk. "I have legal experience."

"I don't see reference to that here."

"Well...I'm divorced, and that involves all kinds of complicated legal paperwork. And I once helped a friend file for bankruptcy."

He closed the portfolio and handed it back to me. "That's not quite what we had in mind. But thank you for stopping by."

The real-estate firm told me they were looking for someone with "less notoriety."

"Don't think of it as notoriety," I said. "Think of it as celebrity. Don't you think having a famous person on staff would draw customers?"

Apparently not.

By three o'clock, the oppressive Houston humidity had wilted my hair and melted my makeup. I had a quarter-size blister from my five-hundred-dollar shoes, a chip in my manicure and a run in my ten-dollar pantyhose. And I still had no job.

I sat in the car with the air conditioner running, trying to plot my next move. I could sign on with a temp agency and be the flavor of the week at a series of jobs where no one would remember my name and I'd never be able to find the ladies' room. I could buy another paper and try the want ads again.

I scowled at my own face, smiling out from the copy of the paper on the seat beside me. A lot of good it had done to bring that along. No one had been impressed by my brief brush with fame.

Who would have thought when I sat down to write a letter to the editor, it would have ended up this way? I remembered the rush I'd had that first day seeing my name in print. It was a feeling I could get used to.

I sat up straighter. If I'd been in a cartoon, a lightbulb would have glowed over my head. Well, why not see my name in print more often? Like—every day?

I put the car in gear and headed down Bellaire Boulevard, toward the offices of the *Houston Banner*.

The glass-and-steel skyscraper overlooking the muddy waters of Brays Bayou might have been an oil-company office or an accounting firm. It didn't look like my idea of a newspaper office. Newspaper offices ought to have men in shirtsleeves barking into old-style, chunky telephone receivers and crusty editors chomping on the ends of cigars. Women in padded suit jackets would hunt and peck at old upright typewriters and reporters would race down the aisle, shouting "Stop the presses."

Okay, so maybe I watch too many old movies. All I saw when I stepped onto the newsroom floor was a row of cubicles filled with glowing computer screens. A woman wearing jeans and a sweatshirt walked past, talking on a cell phone, and a guy with a ponytail was intent on a game of computer solitaire.

A receptionist looked up from her computer. "May I help you?"

"I'm here to see the editor," I said.

She did that thing they must teach in receptionist school—you know, that expression where they raise their eyebrows at you and stare down their noses at the same time. "Do you have an appointment?"

"I'm here about the consumer columnist's job."

"I'm not aware of any interviews scheduled for that position."

I pretended I was Katharine Hepburn in *Woman of the Year* and gave her what I hoped was a supremely confident look. "Then maybe he forgot to tell you." My smile was purposely insincere. "Would you just tell him that Phoebe Frame is here."

While she muttered into the phone, I wandered farther into the room. The guy playing solitaire glanced up at me. "Are you winning?" I asked.

He shook his head. "I never do."

"The secret is to cheat."

"How do you—"

"Miss Frame? I'm Gus Sanborn, managing editor."

Still playing Katharine Hepburn, I held out my hand. "I spoke to you on the phone a few weeks ago, Mr. Sanborn. You mentioned that your consumer reporter, Simon Saler, had taken another position as a sports writer."

He shook my hand and frowned. "That's right. Man still doesn't know the difference between a backdoor slider and a Baltimore chop."

"I'd like to apply for the position," I said.

"Do you know the difference between a backdoor slider and a Baltimore chop?"

I blinked. "Um, is a Baltimore chop anything like a pork chop?" I struggled to get back into Katharine Hepburn mode. "Actually, I want to apply to be your new consumer reporter."

He looked me up and down, not in a sexual way, but more as if he was measuring me for a straitjacket. "Just what makes you think you can do the job?"

I opened my portfolio and extracted the article about me. "When you told me you didn't have a consumer reporter to help me, I went after Easy Motors by myself. And I won."

His eyes widened and he looked at me again. "You're the chick with the bumper stickers?"

I smiled. "That's me. So you see, I have a proven consumer victory under my belt. And something of a reputation with your readers."

He motioned me past the row of cubicles to a glassed-in office. "Have a seat. You want some coffee?"

I sat on the edge of a plain wooden chair. "No, thank you."

"It's terrible stuff anyway." He poured a cup and settled behind the desk. "Do you have any journalism experience, Ms. Frame?"

I shook my head. "But I can type ninety-five words a minute."

He winced. "It might not seem like it sometimes, but writing generally involves more than just typing."

I flushed. "Oh, I know that. I just meant that I'm familiar with computers and different programs and things. As for the writing part, well, you printed my letter to the editor, about my problem with my car."

He nodded thoughtfully. "Our readers liked that letter. The whole underdog story."

"And that illustrates how I have a creative approach to problem solving. And I'm not afraid to stick my neck out to help someone."

He laughed. "I'll say that." He tapped the portfolio. "What about the job you have now?"

I made myself sit still and not squirm in my chair. I'd prepared for this question. "I quit because I wanted to pursue a job that allowed for more interaction with the public."

He leaned back in his chair and studied me a long moment. "Maybe we could give you a try. Let you write a few columns, see how it goes over."

"Yes!" I jumped up and leaned across the desk. "I'll do a great job. You won't regret hiring me."

He rose also, holding up his hands as if he was afraid any moment now I'd launch myself at him. "Now, I'm not promising anything. This is just a trial."

I nodded. "I understand. But you'll see. I'll do great."

"All right. Well, ask Lisa to show you the way to the personnel office. You can start Monday."

I practically danced out of his office. The man playing solitaire looked up as I passed. "I never look that happy when I come out of Sanborn's office," he said.

"It's this magical effect I have on men."

At the stunned look on his face, I laughed and floated away. I did feel magical. No more losing for me. This time, Phoebe Frame was a winner. And I'd fight anybody who tried to take that away from me.

JEFF PICKED ME UP AT THE HOUSE Friday evening, since we'd agreed we shouldn't take a chance on someone seeing my car parked at the clinic after hours. I met him at the door dressed in black jeans, a black sleeveless sweater and black boots. "You look like a cat burglar," he said.

I brushed my hands along my thighs. "I didn't want to be conspicuous. After all, I'm not supposed to be at the office."

"But we don't have to break in. I have a key, remember?"

He took my arm and walked me to his truck. "I'm not complaining, though. You look cute." He opened the passenger door, then pinched my butt as I climbed into the seat.

See, I told myself. He's not serious. This is just a game to him.

I hadn't been to the office in five days and already it seemed like a strange place to me. The rooms were eerily quiet, lit only by the greenish glow of battery chargers and emergency lighting. Someone had put out the Thanksgiving decorations: sheafs of wheat and cornstalks, cutouts of turkeys and pilgrims. Albert grinned at us from beneath a Pilgrim's hat and wide white collar.

Jeff locked the front door behind us and we headed for Patterson's office. He switched on the desk lamp and ran his hand across the edge of the giant wooden desk. "I remember the last time we were here together," he said.

I swallowed, heart thudding like a bass drum. I remembered, too. "Um, we have work to do," I reminded him.

He smiled, and switched on the computer. "Okay, what do you want me to do?"

"Find the visuals for Patterson's talk tomorrow and insert these." I pulled the transparencies out of an envelope I was carrying.

Jeff held them up to the light and let out a low whistle. "The audience ought to get a kick out of this."

"I always heard it was important to incorporate humor into a speech."

He laid the transparencies on the table. "Patterson won't think it's funny. And we'll need to scan them."

"I already had that done." I handed him a disk.

He took the disk and tapped it against his hand. "We could both get in big trouble for this."

"Maybe, but do you really think Patterson's going to want this in court?" I straightened. "Besides, he deserves to get his after all the women he's degraded and used."

He slipped the disk into the drive. "That's one thing I like about you, Phoebe. You don't let people step on you."

"I used to. I guess I got tired of it."

While Jeff worked, I wandered around the office. I swiped a mini Snickers bar from Barb's stash in her desk and looked for more underwear in Joan's office, but didn't find anything interesting.

My workroom had already been converted back to a storage closet. I looked at the stacks of file boxes and shuddered. Was I ever glad to be out of this place. What had kept me hidden back here so long?

Jeff came up behind me and slipped his arms around my waist. "I'm all done. Want to try out that gurney?"

"I've got a better idea."

He nuzzled my neck. "I'm listening."

"Why don't you come home with me?"

He raised his head and his eyes met mine. "To your house? To a real bed and everything?"

I nodded. "I think it's time we take this relationship to the next level, don't you?"

He didn't say another word, just took my hand and pulled me toward the door. My heart hammered in my chest as I followed him to the elevator. I hadn't had a man in my bed since Steve left. I was glad Jeff was going to be the first, but also terribly nervous. Not just about all the normal things—will he think I look fat, will he hate my decor, will he snore? I was scared shitless about what this move meant.

Wanting to bring Jeff home didn't mean I was in love with him or anything, did it?

We got to my house and I stood in the living room, not knowing what to do next. "Uh, would you like a drink?" I asked.

He shook his head. "No, I want to see the bedroom."

"The bedroom?" My voice actually came out as a squeak.

"That's right." He took my hand and pulled me toward the hall. "It's this way, isn't it?"

Luck was definitely with me, since not only was the bed made, but just the day before I'd picked up a week's worth of shoes and shoved them in the closet. I lingered in the doorway while Jeff turned on the lamp on the bedside table. He looked around, saying nothing. Finally, I couldn't stand it anymore. "Do you like it?"

His smile made me weak at the knees. "It's got a bed. It's got you. What's not to like?"

He crossed the room again and started kissing me, his hand reaching up under my sweater. I felt the rush of cool air across my back as the fabric lifted, and the heat of his hand against my ribs. "You're shaking," he said, his mouth against my mouth.

"I'm a little nervous."

"Why?" He looked into my eyes with real concern.

"I'm scared of being hurt." Again. I didn't add the last part, but it was there. I felt faint. This honesty thing was scary.

"I'm not going to hurt you, Phoebe." He stroked the side of my cheek. "I care too much about you to ever hurt you."

There went another cold place inside me, melting away.

I care about you, too, Jeff. So much. I couldn't say it yet, but I thought it. Loudly. I hope he got the message.

I took his hand and led him over to the bed. The way he looked in my eyes, I think he did get the message.

21

THE ANNUAL TEXAS MEDICAL Association Conference was the largest gathering of physicians in the Southwest. What with the various auxiliaries, vendors and doctors' spouses in attendance, over a thousand people filled the halls of the Albert Thomas Convention Center in downtown Houston.

So it was easy enough for me to slip in along with Jeff. He was an official vendor and had made up a fake badge designating me as his assistant. All I had to do was avoid being seen by anyone who might recognize me until it was time for Patterson's speech.

Patterson's talk was listed on the program as The Family Physician and Antibiotics: Are We Using Our Best Weapons Effectively? Jeff and I got to the auditorium early and placed neatly lettered Reserved placards on five chairs directly in front of the speaker's podium. The computer-operated slide projector was already set up, so Jeff had a chance to check out the equipment. "It should work perfectly," he said when he joined me by a side door to the auditorium.

I shifted from one foot to the other. "I think I'm going to be sick."

He patted my arm. "It's going to be fine."

How could he be so sure? I excused myself to go to the ladies' room. If my stomach did decide to give in to this queasiness, I'd just as soon it didn't happen in public.

The ladies' room was around the corner from the auditorium where Patterson was scheduled to give his presentation.

I'd almost reached it when a familiar voice distracted me. "Yes, I'm quite honored to be asked to speak," Patterson boomed.

I turned and saw the good doctor addressing a crowd of admirers. He looked especially dignified today, with a wine-red silk handkerchief in his breast pocket and a matching silk tie. He looked like the kind of doctor you'd trust to put your interests first. The kind of doctor you'd see on a TV show, lingering at the bedside of a dying patient.

Which just goes to show that, for some people, image really is everything.

"Dr. Patterson, what advice would you give our readers concerning antibiotics?" A reporter, notebook in hand, had her pen poised to record Patterson's answer.

I couldn't really see the woman, but Patterson's smile told me she was young and probably good-looking. "Well, my dear, I would say it's important to be informed as to your options, and also to find a physician you can trust. I'd be happy to discuss the subject with you further after my talk. Perhaps over cocktails?"

I ducked into the bathroom and into a stall. Instead of fighting nausea, I was battling panic. Who was I kidding to think I could fight a man like Patterson? Not only did he have all his colleagues snowed, now he had the press eating out of his hand. What I was doing wasn't going to make any difference to him, and it would probably amount to social suicide for me.

I looked up at the ad board mounted on the inside of the stall door, as if hoping to find inspiration in notices about diet pills and local radio stations. An almost naked woman smiled out at me from an ad for a prominent plastic surgeon. "Be yourself, only better," the ad proclaimed.

Below it was a stark black-and-white notice. Are you a battered woman? it asked. Call for help, and then a phone number.

I stared at those harsh words, then my eyes flickered back to the model in the plastic-surgery ad. That pretty much summed up everything, didn't it? All those subtle messages women get every day that we aren't quite good enough the way we are. And how often do we take that stuff in without a protest?

Here was my chance to make my own protest. How could I let this opportunity get away from me? I might get lucky and make a difference to somebody. Maybe even to myself.

By the time I got back to Jeff, the auditorium was filling up. Several people approached the reserved chairs and looked at them curiously, but no one said anything or made any objections. It's amazing what people will stand for if you make it look official enough.

Patterson arrived with a group of doctors who wore beribboned speakers' badges and the room grew quiet. The president of the TMA introduced Patterson with a lot of flowery praise about his expertise as a physician, etc. And that was all true. Patterson was a good doctor. He just let his personality and the way he treated his employees taint his medical skills.

Patterson stood and acknowledged the applause, then shuffled through his notes. While he was doing that, I opened the side door and let in my partners in crime: four women, all obviously quite pregnant. They wore sunglasses and big coats and made a great show of waddling to the reserved seats in the front row, where I joined them. Jeff waited by the door, ready to help us make a quick getaway.

A murmur rolled through the audience, and I thought I heard a few chuckles. Patterson stared down at us and blanched. He looked over his shoulder, perhaps for someone to remove us, but no one came to his rescue.

After a tense moment, he cleared his throat and began his

talk. "A study by Doern, et al, of one thousand, six hundred and one clinical isolates of *Streptococcus pneumoniae* showed the overall rate of strains showing resistance to penicillin at 29.5 percent, while 17.4 percent..."

I tell you, it was all I could do to keep my eyes open, but the audience was attentive enough. Though I sensed that more than a few of them were watching our little group in the front row.

"I have some slides to illustrate my points," Patterson said, and nodded for the projector to be switched on.

With an audible whir, the first slide appeared on the screen. It was a petri dish full of some sort of ugly growth. Gross, if you asked me, but the way the audience reacted, you'd have thought a photo of Linda Evangelista had flashed on the screen.

By this time, Patterson had relaxed. He knew he had everyone's attention. I imagine he was already congratulating himself on making such a good showing.

"And here we have an illustration of *Streptococcus pneumoniae* after inoculation with ciprofloxacin."

The projector clicked and a gasp rose from the audience like a cloud of steam. A woman's picture, a black bar concealing her eyes, popped up. The woman was extremely pregnant, and the typed legend under her photo read: I was seduced by Dr. Ken Patterson.

Patterson reddened, and clicked a button to fast-forward. Another woman's face appeared. Also pregnant, her caption read: I lost my job when Dr. Ken Patterson dumped me.

Frantic, Patterson clicked again. Another woman appeared. And then another. All pregnant, all confessing to affairs with Dr. Ken Patterson that had ended badly.

The room was so loud now, no one could hear Patterson's protests over the laughter and shouted questions. I nodded to my companions and we all stood and walked down the center aisle and out of the room.

Or rather, I walked. The other women did the exaggerated duck walk of the extremely pregnant, their bellies stuck out in front of them. They'd slipped out of the coats and now everyone could see the T-shirts they wore that read, I'm a Product of Managed Care.

Someone started booing, and others joined in. Two female physicians stood and were soon joined by others, men and women. Patterson put his hands to his head, as if to ward off blows. Head bowed, he scurried off the stage. The slides continued to flash overhead. Woman after woman. I was seduced by Dr. Ken Patterson.

Outside, the women and I ducked into the ladies' room while Jeff kept watch. We emerged minutes later, having shed the T-shirts and the pregnancy bellies I'd borrowed from Jerry Armbruster. Then we made a dash for a side entrance and Jeff's waiting truck.

"I don't know when I've had more fun." Kathleen, my predecessor as an object of Patterson's affections, hugged me. "Thanks for letting me in on this."

The other women agreed, and we exchanged hugs all around and promises to keep in touch. Finally, Jeff and I were alone. He shook his head. "What do you think they're doing to him right now?"

"I don't know, but I'm going to find out." I headed back toward the building.

Jeff grabbed my arm. "What, are you crazy? People will recognize you. You could be mobbed."

"I didn't do all this work, take all this risk, not to see how things turned out." I shook him off. "Call me vindictive, but I want to see Patterson roast."

It wasn't hard to locate the doctor. All I had to do was follow the sound of shouting. He was cornered in a room just off the auditorium, the press hurling questions at him. "Doctor, who were those women?" "Doctor, is it true you had all those affairs?" "Doctor, do you feel you've violated the public's trust in you as a professional?"

Patterson stammered denials, but the questions continued. The suit that had looked so dapper only moments before now seemed to hang on his frame, and his tan, handsome face looked pale and old.

"Anderson! Barclay! You know me. Tell these people that I'm a good man. These accusations have no basis in fact." He beseeched his colleagues for help. The other doctors looked embarrassed. One shook his head in a pitying gesture, then they turned their backs and left him to the wolves.

Some of the reporters turned to watch the other doctors leave, and that's when someone spotted me. "Isn't that one of them? The woman who was sitting with the pregnant women?"

The press corps surged toward me with such suddenness I was afraid I'd be crushed. I turned toward the door to get the hell out of there, but Patterson's voice stopped me. "She did this to get back at me for refusing her advances!" he shouted. "She had a crush on me and I refused her. She became obsessed with me, until I had no choice but to let her go. This is all about revenge. There's no truth in it."

"Is it true?" a reporter asked. "Did you work for Dr. Patterson?"

I tried to read the expressions on the reporters' faces, to see if they believed Patterson's accusations. One or two looked skeptical, but most were more guarded, waiting for my answer. "I did work for Ken Patterson," I said. "And he did recently ask me to leave his employment."

A murmur rose up among the press corps, and I had to raise my voice to continue. "He asked me to leave because I had repeatedly turned down his advances. That's his pattern.

He has an affair with an employee, or tries to, and if she refuses him or he grows tired of her, he fires her or persuades her to quit. You can check his employment records and see the truth."

"Lies!" Patterson shouted, but the reporters ignored him.

"Weren't you in the paper recently about your car?" one asked. "Francis something or other?"

"It's Phoebe. Phoebe Frame." I leaned forward to speak into his microphone. "I'm the new consumer reporter for the *Houston Banner*."

"Ms. Frame! Ms. Frame!" They clamored for my attention. I smiled, some of my nervousness replaced by elation. They were really listening to me. I had made a difference.

"Phoebe, you've already taken on a crooked used-car dealer," a woman said. "Is this exposure of Dr. Patterson an example of the kind of in-your-face reporting we can expect from you in the future?"

I blinked. No one had ever called me "in-your-face" before. I cleared my throat and leaned forward to address them again. Sometimes words come to you, you know? Like a gift. The moment arrives and, for once, you know just what to say. I looked out at those reporters and gave them my best smile. "I think it's safe to say that the only thing you can plan on expecting from me in the future is the unexpected."

22

Darla and Tony decided to have their wedding at the All Faiths Wedding Chapel on Westheimer, mainly because it was close to the Knights of Columbus Hall where they'd booked their reception. The KCs won out over the Sons of Hermann when they agreed to give the happy couple a discount if they let the Knights use their Elvis-themed decorations for their next Friday night dance.

So, on a sunny afternoon in November, I found myself helping my hairdresser and best friend arrange her hair for her wedding, while strains of "Loving You" drifted from the adjacent chapel. "Do you think the sequins on the veil are too much?" Darla tugged at the sequin-studded netting that cascaded from a daisy crown pinned to her hair.

"Too much" is a relative term at an Elvis wedding. What with the minister in a white jumpsuit, decorations which included flashing Christmas lights, guitars and stuffed hound dogs, and an Elvis impersonator crooning "Don't Be Cruel" to the wedding guests, a sequined veil hardly seemed worth noting. "You look fine." I straightened the veil over her shoulders. "Beautiful."

She frowned into the mirror. "I don't know. Do you think it makes me look like I have measles?"

"No. Besides, it will be lifted for the pictures."

"That's right." She looked relieved. "I keep forgetting all these details."

"I warned you. Wedding days give you amnesia."

"Darla? Are you ready yet?" Darla's mother, wearing an aqua-and-silver formal, her white hair piled into a beehive, stuck her head into the room. "Tony's starting to look nervous."

"We're ready, Mama. Go ahead and take your seat." Darla turned to me. "Can you believe I'm doing this?"

"It's going to be wonderful." I hugged her, taking care not to crush her hair. "Come on. Let's go."

Darla's father, who had grown his sideburns long for the occasion, was waiting in the hall. I followed him and Darla to the foyer and checked my dress one last time in the mirror while we waited for our cue to go in. After looking at half a dozen chiffon numbers in eye-achingly bright sherbet colors, we'd settled on this pink-sequined minidress with white go-go boots. Retro, but not too ridiculous.

The first notes of the "Hawaiian Wedding Song" sounded. "That's your cue!" Darla hissed.

I settled my single white magnolia on my stomach and began my stutter-step up the aisle. Talk about a weird feeling. The last time I'd done this, I'd been a bride myself. My stomach had the same jittery feeling I'd had back then. Mainly, I was afraid I'd lose a heel or trip, and go sprawling down the aisle, magnolia petals flying. I took a deep breath and focused on the blinking white lights over the altar. Tony had wanted to string the lights in the shape of a guitar, but the chapel had drawn the line at that.

At last, I reached the end of the aisle, and took my place across from Tony. His head shone in the bright lights, and his dark sideburns made him look more like a pirate than Elvis, but he was appropriately misty eyed as the music switched to the "Wedding March" and Darla and her father started down the aisle. At one point, he even wiped his eyes on the sleeve of his leather jacket.

The minister stepped forward, the rhinestones on his white

jumpsuit winking in the light. "Dearly beloved, we are gathered here..."

Amazingly enough, considering the circumstances, the wedding vows were straightforward, with not one reference to "baby." Tony's hand shook as he slipped the wedding band on Darla's finger, and my own eyes got moist when he lifted the veil and kissed her. I hastily blotted the tears with my fingers, hoping I wouldn't end up looking like a raccoon.

"Ladies and gentlemen, may I present Mr. and Mrs. Tony Bosco."

As the Elvis impersonator crooned "Love Me Tender," the happy couple hurried down the aisle and into their waiting pink Cadillac for the ride to the reception.

I followed the Caddie to the hall and had scarcely stepped out of my Mustang when a round, pasty-faced man in a red beret accosted me. "Are you Phoebe? Phoebe Frame?"

I eyed him warily. In addition to the beret, he had a thin moustache, so thin it looked as if he'd drawn it in with an eyebrow pencil. "Who are you?"

"Henry." Only he said it "On-ree" with a stuffy French accent. "The caterer."

"Caterer" seemed a lofty term for the man Darla had found to make ten dozen peanut-butter-and-banana sandwiches, crusts removed, cut in fourths, as well as a gallon of fried pickles and a cake in the shape of a guitar. "What's the problem, Henry?" I pronounced it the good old Texas way.

"The plumbing, it is backed up."

"You mean the sink's stopped up?"

He shook his head. "No, I mean the facilities don't work."

"The facilities?" I frowned. "What facilities?"

"The toilet's stopped up!" His face was as red as the beret now and the fake French accent had succumbed to a strong Texas twang.

A group of well-dressed wedding guests stopped on their

way across the parking lot to stare. "Gee whiz, Henry, what's the big deal?" I said. "Grab a plunger."

I started toward the hall and he fell into step beside me. "It's going to take more than a plunger to fix this," he said. "And I've got two kegs of beer set up. This could turn into a major crisis."

Which just goes to show that there's no such thing as a perfect wedding. It's sort of like that old expression "nature abhors a vacuum." Seems to me nature doesn't care much for man-made perfection, either. Give her a bunch of people trying to put together a perfect anything—from a picnic in the park to a multithousand-dollar wedding—and nature will throw in a thunderstorm, hurricane or infestation of fire ants just to show who's boss.

Or in this case, plumbing problems. The men's room was not a pretty sight. And when I checked out the ladies' room on the other side of the wall that divided the two facilities I found out it wasn't in much better shape. "What are you going to do?" Henry asked.

What kind of a consumer advocate was I, not to mention what kind of friend, if I let a mess like this ruin my friend's wedding?

"What are you going to do?" Henry asked again.

I started digging through my purse, looking for a business card I'd stuck there weeks ago. "I'm going to call a plumber," I said.

"You won't get a plumber to come out here on a Saturday afternoon," Henry said.

I pulled out a rectangle of pasteboard and stared at the slogan written there. "This one will." Vince Zaragosa said he couldn't mend broken hearts, but he could certainly prevent one if he got out here right away.

I pulled out my phone and dialed. "Hello, Mrs. Zaragosa, is Mr. Zaragosa there? I have a big favor to ask...."

THIRTY MINUTES LATER, Vince Zaragosa was up to his elbows in plumbing hell, and I was serving up plates of hors d'oeuvres and slices of the guitar-shaped cake, along with red soda water, champagne and beer. I'd promised Vince all the cake and peanut-butter sandwiches he could eat, and free beer, if he'd come over here, but all I really had to do was mention that he'd be saving a wedding reception and he'd promised to be right over. The big romantic.

The reception music was all Elvis, all the time. Tony and Darla danced to "Can't Help Falling in Love," then segued into "Jailhouse Rock." Then Jeff danced with Darla. I watched the two of them sway to "Any Way You Want Me." Darla hadn't stopped smiling all afternoon and when she looked up at Jeff and laughed, a longing so painful it brought tears to my eyes made me drop my cake server and back away from the buffet table. I wanted to be the one in Jeff's arms, dancing at our own wedding.

Thoughts like that are nothing short of dangerous, so I decided I'd better take a break and try to pull myself together. Obviously, all this hearts-and-flowers stuff was messing with my head.

I handed my cake server over to one of Darla's cousins and retreated to a back room the KCs had dubbed the "ladies' parlor," where I'd stashed my purse. I dug out my makeup kit and touched up my mascara, but while I was standing there staring at my reflection in the mirror, I burst into tears.

"I know it's sort of tradition to cry at weddings, but you're supposed to do it in the church, not afterward at the reception."

I jumped as Vince Zaragosa emerged from the little bathroom that opened into the parlor. I sniffed and tried to wipe away tears with my fingers. "I guess I just get emotional at these things."

He handed me a snowy-white handkerchief. "Anything I can do to help?"

I sniffed and wiped away fresh tears. "Not unless you've changed your policy on broken hearts."

He settled himself on the edge of the chair, somehow looking right at home in his overalls and tool belt amongst the Louis XIV chairs and sofas. "So who broke your heart? I could fix his toilets so they never work right."

I smiled through the tears and shook my head. "It's not exactly broken. Maybe just...bruised." I took a deep breath. "I made a mistake once before and now I'm scared I'll make another one. So scared I won't let the one guy who seems to really care about me get too close."

He rested his elbows on his knees and clasped his hands together. "If this were one of them TV shows my wife gets all mushy over, this is the place where I'd offer you some kind of wise advice."

I waited for more, but when it didn't come, I said, "But you're not?"

He shrugged. "Not everything is a matter of following code and plugging up leaks. Sometimes there aren't any right answers. Or wrong ones. Sometimes you have to operate on instinct."

I frowned. "I don't know if my instincts are any good anymore."

He leaned over and patted my knee. "Yes, you do. You just have to get out of the way and pay attention. Sometimes you have to stop thinking with your head and leap with your heart."

A knock on the door startled us. Jeff stuck his head in the room and smiled at me. "There you are. Somebody told me they thought they'd seen you duck in here."

I managed a weak smile and stood. "Jeff, this is Mr. Zaragosa, the man who's saved this reception by agreeing to come out here on a Saturday to get the bathrooms working again. Mr. Zaragosa, this is Jeff Fischer."

The two of them shook hands, then Jeff turned to me. "I came to see if you'd dance with me."

The scared rabbit part of me wanted to say no, but another voice, deeper down inside, said to let this happen, however things played out. I took his hand and nodded. "I'd like that."

We left Mr. Zaragosa in the parlor. When I looked back over my shoulder at him, he smiled and nodded, as if he, at least, thought I was doing the right thing.

"You make a lovely go-go girl," Jeff said as we walked back toward the reception hall.

"I drew the line at bubble hair," I said. "But the boots are kind of a kick, aren't they?"

"You're a kick, Phoebe Frame." He led me onto the dance floor, where we slow-danced to "A Fool Such As I." I told myself it was part of the whole wedding magic, or maybe just the effects of two glasses of champagne, but I never wanted to move out of his arms.

Eventually, we did leave the dance floor and made our way back to the buffet tables. Jeff was pouring more champagne when a toddler in a frilly dress bumped up against his leg. He smiled down at her. "What's up, munchkin?"

"Daddy?" She stuck her finger in her mouth and looked around, eyes searching.

Jeff kneeled down. "Did you lose your daddy?"

She nodded and her little chin quivered.

"Awww, don't cry." He gathered her up in his arms and stood. "I'm sure we can find him."

I watched, astonished. Jeff looked so...so comfortable with that baby in his arms. So strong, and masculine and...sexy. What happened to the man in the bowling alley who hadn't wanted anything to do with children?

We didn't go far before a worried-looking man came rushing up to us. "Daddy!" the little girl crowed, and held her arms out to him.

"Amanda, what did I tell you about wandering off?" The man took her from Jeff, and pulled her close. "Thanks," he said to us, then headed back toward his table across the room.

Jeff had a pleased expression on his face. "What a cutie, huh?"

"I thought you didn't like children," I said.

He looked at me, one eyebrow raised. "Whatever gave you that idea?"

"In the bowling alley that day—you complained about those children running around."

"I don't like misbehaving children, but, as individuals, I don't have anything against them." He smiled. "I even like some of them."

We joined the other guests on the steps and helped send the newlyweds off to a honeymoon in Las Vegas with a shower of soap bubbles. "Who would have thought anything so tacky could actually be so beautiful?" I sniffed and replaced my bubble wand in the tulle-wrapped bottle.

Jeff handed me a handkerchief. "I'm sure it's a wedding no one here will ever forget."

He slipped his arm around me and together we walked back into the reception hall. "Why don't we go somewhere this evening and celebrate the happy couple?"

I glanced up at him. "You mean, another date?"

He grinned. "I could get used to it. How about you?"

I hesitated, then nodded. "I think maybe I could."

"So where do you want to go?"

I thought a moment, then smiled at the wonderful idea that popped into my head. "Do you ice-skate?"

IT TURNED OUT JEFF DIDN'T KNOW HOW to ice-skate. But he didn't tell me that until we were actually out on the ice. The first time he let go of the rail, his feet slid out from under him and, arms windmilling, he crashed to the ice.

"Are you all right?" I tugged on his arm, trying to help him up.

"I think my pride's hurt more than anything." He climbed up me until he was standing again, though he still clung to my arm. "Although my backside smarts pretty good."

"Why didn't you tell me you don't know how to skate?"

"I could tell you really wanted to go." He grinned. "Besides, I thought it might be fun if you taught me."

Note to any men out there who might be inclined to pay attention: there is something incredibly sexy about a strong man who is just a little bit vulnerable.

In any case, I got all warm and gushy inside when Jeff asked me to teach him to ice-skate, and immediately became determined to turn him into the next Elvis Stojko.

Unfortunately, there was one minor flaw in this plan: Jeff didn't have any talent. I might as well have tried to teach a bull to roller-skate. He tried, I'll give him that. But every time I let go of him, his ankles wobbled, his knees buckled and his arms flailed. I figured it was only a matter of time before he broke something.

Finally, he sagged against the railing. "This isn't any fun for you," he said. "Why don't you skate by yourself for a while? I'll watch."

"Are you sure?" I backed away from him. "You won't pout?"

He laughed. "Why would I pout?"

"Steve always pouted when we went anywhere and I left him alone. He said he felt like an idiot standing there by himself."

"That's because Steve is an idiot. Now go on. Show me your stuff."

Slowly at first, then gaining speed, I skated around the

rink. "Dancing Queen" began playing over the loudspeaker, and I was immediately transported back in time to those long Saturdays when Darla and I would spend hours at this rink. My hair streamed out behind me and the blades of my skates cut into the ice in time to the music. My thighs burned with the effort and my ankles began to ache, but I didn't want to stop. Soaring around the ice was the next best thing to flying. Why had I ever given that up?

I rounded the corner and saw Jeff across the rink. He'd gotten off the ice and was standing at the rail, leaning over it, watching me, a smile on his face that made me feel weightless and full of energy. When I was almost in front of him, I tried a spin, a graceful pirouette that had once been my specialty. I twirled, faster and faster, the world a colorful blur at the edge of my vision. Then I began to slow, and everything gradually came back into focus: the other skaters gliding past, the neon of the store signs and Jeff's smiling face.

"That was really good," he said, coming to meet me as I stepped off the ice.

"Thanks." I was puffing, breathless from the exertion.

"That twirl thing you did—it looked like something you'd see in the Olympics."

I laughed. "Olympic skaters learn that kind of thing when they're still in elementary school."

"Well, it looked pretty impressive to me."

"When I was in high school, my friends and I would wear short skirts and we'd twirl like that so the boys could see our underwear."

"And they say men are the sexual aggressors." He gestured toward the ice. "Do you want to skate some more?"

I shook my head. "I think I want to get some coffee."

We bought lattes at a Starbucks that overlooked the ice rink. I sank down into my chair with a sigh. "Tired?" Jeff asked.

I nodded. "I'd forgotten how much work goes into getting ready for a wedding."

"Speaking of work, I stopped by the medical clinic this morning, on my way to the chapel."

"Oh?" Last I'd heard, Patterson had taken a sabbatical from practice, but I didn't know anything else.

"They've got a new doctor there," Jeff said. "I stopped by because she wants to put the transcription system back in."

"She?"

He nodded. "The staff is happy and I think the clinic managers hope a woman will be better, PR-wise."

I laughed. "So I guess they're looking for a transcriptionist."

"Are you interested in your old job back?"

I shook my head. "No, thanks. I like my new job."

He leaned forward. "I haven't had a chance to tell you, but what you did with Patterson took guts. I'm proud of you."

Are there many sweeter words in the English language? From the time we're toddlers being potty trained, we're always listening for those words from someone: our parents, our spouses, our friends. "I love you" gets tossed around so casually sometimes, but to be told you've made someone proud, now that's really special.

I touched my cup to his. "You know what the best thing is?" I asked. "I'm proud of myself."

"Looks like things have turned out pretty well for you."

I nodded. "I wouldn't have said it six months ago, but I think now this divorce has been the best thing that ever happened to me. It forced me to really look at my life and to try new things."

He reached across the table and took my hand in his. "Do I fit in there somewhere?"

I turned to watch the skaters on the ice. A little girl scooted by, holding tightly to her father's hand. One of these days, she'd be brave enough to let go of that hand and soar across the ice, so free.

I was feeling brave today. I turned to look at Jeff again. "What would you say if I told you I've fallen in love with you?"

Everything went still for a moment. Neither one of us blinked and the sounds of the ice rink and the mall faded away. I watched Jeff, scared to move, scared to breathe even.

Then the most wonderful smile spread over his face. Across his lips and up to his eyes. A smile that came from somewhere in his soul. "I'd say you'd made me a very happy man." He leaned forward and kissed me—a sweet, gentle touching of our lips. "I love you, Phoebe Frame," he said. "Don't you ever forget it."

I smiled at him, and at the reflection of my own happiness in his eyes. "I won't forget."

We kissed again, a long, slow kiss that said all the things I hadn't found words for yet. I held on to the advice Mr. Zaragosa had given me, and vowed to try leaping with my heart, even if sometimes it felt like skydiving without a parachute.